For All Seasons

A Collection of Stories and
Reflections.

Bala Mudaly

Tale

Some names and identifying details have been omitted or changed to protect the privacy of individuals.

Cover design by Robert New

Copyright: Every effort has been made to trace copyright holders or use works in the public domain.

First Published 2022
Copyright © 2022 Bala Mudaly
All rights reserved.

National Library of Australia Cataloguing-in-Publication entry:
Creator: Mudaly, Bala, author.
Title: For All Seasons: A Collection of Stories and Reflections.

ISBN: 978-0-6480386-5-8

Tale Publishing
Melbourne, Victoria

Tale

To everything
There is a season
And a time to every purpose, under heaven
Ecclesiastes 3

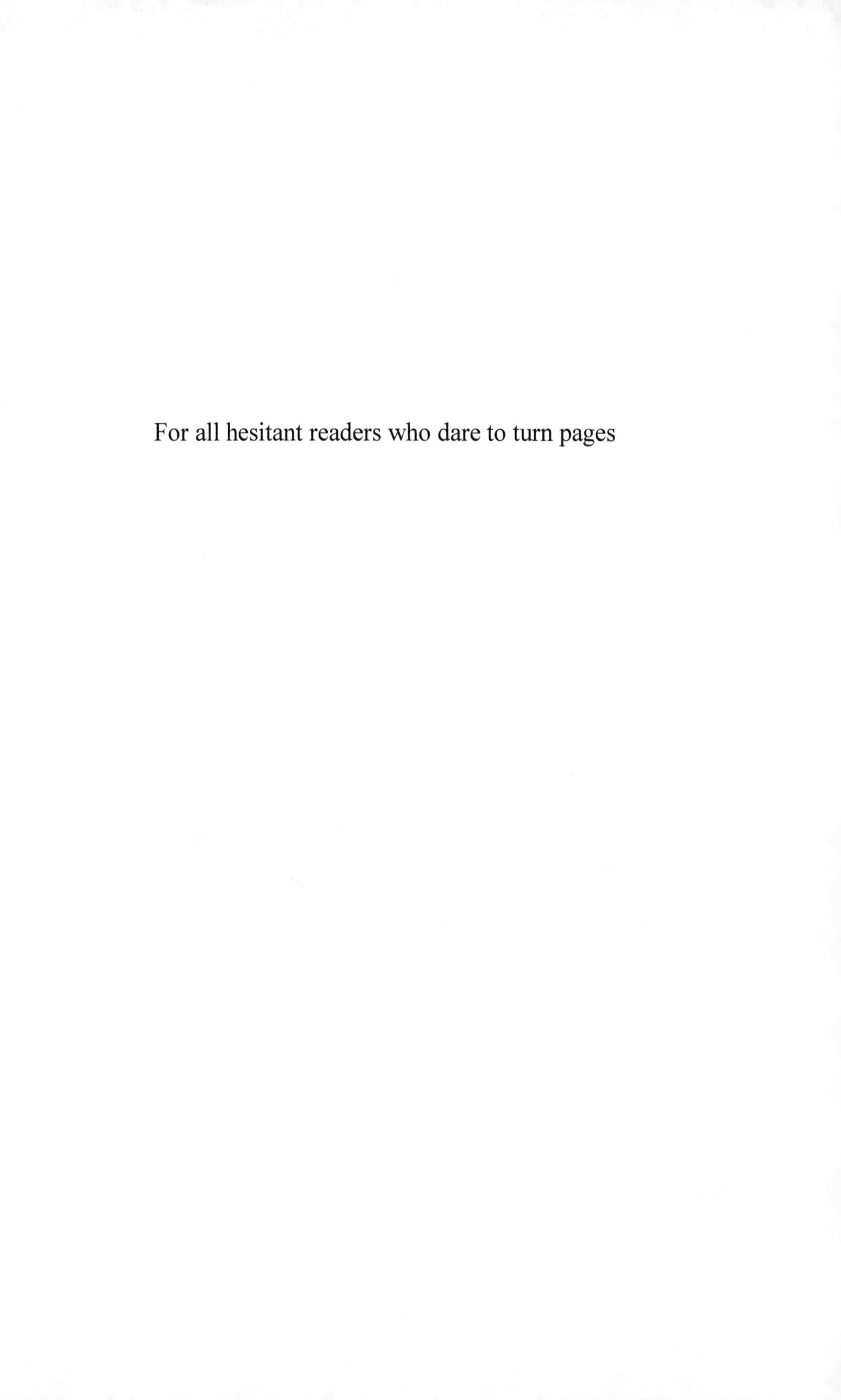

For all hesitant readers who dare to turn pages

Foreword
by
Chris Goddard

After reading *For All Seasons* for the first time, I went to one of my favourite places in Melbourne to reflect on the wonderful and quirky book that I had just read. There is a billabong, filled by the Yarra River, a peaceful place just a few kilometres from the city centre. The reflections of the eucalypts on the water are beautiful, disturbed only by the wonderful water birds.

Reflections in all their forms have always fascinated me. One of my earliest memories of them is being asked by a teacher at school what it was that everyone else in the room could do and I could not. He explained that everyone else in the room could see me but that I could not. I could only see a reflection of myself if I were given a mirror. The teacher told us that William Shakespeare had written about this in *Julius Caesar*.

This book is full of the most wonderful reflections on a life lived in many different landscapes. Landscapes shape us. Bala describes eloquently and in many ways the landscapes that have shaped him and his entire life. He reflects on Apartheid and Covid, on South Africa and his Melbourne neighbours, on toilets (sorry Bala, lavatories) in the air and in the ground, on Buddhism, sweeping leaves and on Gandhi. Bala's reflections come in many forms: "creative" non-fiction, fiction and poetry. The reflections shine brightly and will illuminate yours as you read them.

Bala takes the reader to many places, amongst them Port Arthur, a place he visited on a cruise ship. Port Arthur, he movingly describes, was home to three tragic stories of death and deprivation. The tourist site and guides emphasise the history of the convict settlement while "glossing over" the other two: the brutal treatment of the indigenous people, and the terrible 1996 massacre in which 35 died and 23 others were wounded.

Bala explains how important books were informing his identity and his understanding of the world he lives in. His first glimpse of a library was on a school outing and the sign "Whites Only" on the door. Later a library for non-whites opened, and at the age of 13 his father enrolled him. Bala writes powerfully of how books shaped him. In South Africa, as in Nazi Germany, many books were banned and burned. He writes of his feelings of "fear and daring" in reading and sharing books that were banned, and the need to whisper furtively in such situations. Bala knew Strini Moodley, the writer and playwright, who was to be charged with and found guilty of terrorism and served five years on Robben Island. Books not only shaped Bala but helped him under-stand the lives of others beyond his ethnic origins, beyond his ethnic horizon, and helped him be-come South African rather than just Indian.

I can confidently say that this wonderful, unusual book will enhance your reflections on your life and the world wherever you are. I can also state that a book such as this would be banned in some countries.

I am privileged to introduce it to you.

Chris Goddard
Adjunct Professor
University of South Australia.
Visiting Professor, University of Hertfordshire

For All Seasons
A Collection of Stories and Reflections.

Creative Non-Fiction

Mallacoota: The Mournings After

Oh bugger, just a 4-seater flying cubbyhouse. No headspace and barely room to breathe. Vincent was on a flight with three other Red Cross volunteers - a recovery support team headed for Mallacoota to help with the aftermath of the devastating bushfires. He was roped in at the last minute by Eve the team leader. She could do with a male on her team, she had explained. Vincent had first met her in Healesville at a Red Cross Emergency Volunteer Training. This was his first deployment. He wiped his flushed face and shaven head with an open palm, hoping his nervousness of wildfires wouldn't be noticed.

~

The engine whirred loud and incessantly making conversation impossible. Since chatting was out, the women spent the time scanning the moving landscape through miniature side-windows. But not Vincent, as heights bothered him.

The plane lurched and swayed as it flew low over hills and valleys, over scorched bush stretching as far as the eye could see, even to the very coastline. The volunteers felt unnerved as they gazed at the devastation caused by an untethered firestorm. 'Awful, awful,' screamed Eve wide-eyed, 'never known anything like this before. Climate change's the culprit.'

The fire had travelled as swiftly as a meteor singeing everything in its path, said a report in the *Herald Sun*. The team sat in frozen silence as the plane circled over the small airfield outside Mallacoota before landing on a relatively short and narrow runway. As it taxied towards the gate and carpark past further scenes of devastation, Vincent had a momentary flashback of Black Saturday. He was on a soccer oval in Marysville, his wife, Anna, near nine months pregnant. They had huddled in the thick of a terrified crowd. The hills all around spurted hellfire and embers. He couldn't stand the screaming and whimpering of the kids as acrid smoke swept over them stinging their eyes and nostrils. He now felt grateful that he hadn't had to go to Mallacoota weeks earlier at the height of the firestorm, in the midst of the trauma and chaos of an evacuation. That would have been a bloody nightmare not unlike Marysville.

~

The Mallacoota Health & Community Hub was where the Red Cross had set up its Relief Centre. The line of tall gums just across the road was little more than charred sentinels. How come then, Vincent and the team wondered, that the fire hadn't consumed this building of mere prefab timber and glass. Mrs Briggs, the Coordinator of the Hub, was there to meet them as they alighted from a Parks Victoria SUV which had collected them from the airport. She caught the looks of amazement on their faces.

'Sheer luck, you know,' she said. 'The wind change was

unexpected like, you see, and the fire took off in another direction.' She pointed to a double-door structure just visible on the far side of the Hub, painted green.

'That's the Men's Shed there. That's where my hubby and his mates were holed up. Scared shit they were. He said the whole thing was quite freakish.' The volunteers nodded in unison.

They'd heard of such bizarre miracles before, in other ferocious bushfires.

~

Just then, two women in Red Cross outfits emerged from the Hub, spotted the new arrivals and rushed to them, all smiles. Hugs and gushing words of welcome followed.

'I'll leave you in their good care, then,' said Mrs Briggs turning to leave. She used a cane for support. 'Make yourselves at home. I'm just across in that building over there if you need anything. Oh, I suppose you'd be attending the community briefing at 6 this evening?' She walked off without expecting a response.

'The worst's just about over, I think,' said Gwen introducing herself as the leader of the volunteers on duty. She spoke with an Irish accent and had a briskness about her as if she had once managed a field hospital.

'Oh, I'm Eve. I take over from you.' Vincent and the two other volunteers said hello, picked up their backpacks and followed Eve and Gwen into the Hub.

While they were chatting with Mrs Briggs a little earlier, several older women had drifted into the Hub.

'Things change rapidly here. Almost daily,' said Bibi who was with Gwen's team. She chose to walk with Vincent and the two women. Vincent waited, but Bibi didn't explain herself.

Something lively seemed to be happening within the building. There was much chatter and laughter.

'It's the older women's sewing club in session,' explained Gwen.

'Yeah?' said Eve raising her eyebrows.

'Yep, there's something on here every day,' added Bibi. 'You'll see.'

'Gosh, speaks of a resilient community, doesn't it?' said Vincent taking a quick peek into the activity hall. 'Back to normality and all that. And so soon? Amazing.'

'Only *seems* that way,' said Bibi, with a quick glance at Vincent.

Did she mean that here too there were others like him, others who attempted to cover up their loss and return to *normal* living? But they weren't like him. Not really. Their experience was recent and very raw, while his grieving went back ten years. It's about time you *pulled yourself together,* mate, his neighbour Bob had urged over a beer. Even his Anna had picked herself up and given herself a new lease of life, thanks to three years of counselling. She was even able to keep her emotions in check when talking about that awful Black Saturday in 2009 when their first child was stillborn.

'It pains me too, dear,' she had said with a sob, easing into his arms. 'Wasn't your fault the ambulance couldn't get through. Can we try again, please?'

~

Soon they all settled around a longish table in the temporary Red Cross room for the handover and debriefing. The room,

with more chairs than needed, was full of Red Cross clutter –
brochures, water bottles, empty coffee cups, laptops and
timetables. Eve and her team were assured by Gwen that they
were not likely to be inundated with people wanting a
sympathetic ear. No. The demand had eased after peaking
two weeks earlier. Whoever turned up now will most likely
ask for Centre Link or the DHHS with offices in the adjacent
building.

~

'What's to be the Red Cross role then?' asked Vincent,
wondering if he hadn't come all this way to breathe toxic air.

'You'll be in recovery mode,' said Gwen. 'Suggest, for a
start, you hang out in the yard at the entrance, greeting
whoever drops by. Casual like. You know what I mean.'

'Yeah. Meet and greet with a friendly face.'

A refrain of *HappyBirthday* filtered in from down the
corridor. Discordant female voices. Boisterous clapping
followed. The volunteers exchanged glances and smiles.
Vincent pushed back his chair and stood up for a stretch. The
others looked up with expectation.

'Okay let's break for a cuppa,' said Gwen. 'I'll show you
folks where to stoke up.'

~

The smoke haze returned like a skulking forest demon. The
warm wind had changed direction once again, blowing over
the lake towards town. Clouds banked rapidly into an
ominous mass.

It was late morning the next day. Vincent was seated on a
bench at the entrance to the Health Care Hub, with a mug of
coffee. A little anxious and unsettled, he wished for company.

A battered and mud-splattered Ute pulled up in the driveway, hesitated a moment before parking. It got the full attention of Vincent. A slight-built, dishevelled man jumped out followed by an agile black spaniel on a leash. The bloke looked about and then headed for the Hub entrance, the spaniel at his heel. He coughed once and grimaced scanning the sky. He pulled on his face mask.

'Not my thing,' he said in a muffled voice. 'Glasses fog up.'

Vincent nodded taking it that the man was speaking to him. 'Yeah,' he said, resting his coffee mug on the bench and getting up. 'I'm Vincent.'

Vincent was in his early 40s, of solid build, almost bald. A carefully manicured moustache accentuated his broad nose and his dusky olive complexion.

'Oh yeah,' said the man dropping his face mask, noting Vincent's red shirt and name tag. 'You with the Red Cross then? Called Damien. Please to meet yeh.'

'Need help?' Vincent inquired casually not wishing to sound intrusive.

'Nah, just here to see the physio. Buggered my hand real bad.' Damien examined his right hand, the thumb all swollen and angry. He looked like a frayed bamboo sapling. Face and arms covered in blotches. But his voice was crisp and strong. Eyes vigilant.

'Serious, eh?' said Vincent.

'I tell yeh mate, it was bloody rough out there. Didn't think we'd make it. Half the bloody day and night tugging at the blasted hose, the jet ripping into the flames, tall as my house. Spot-fires everywhere, flames leaping, leaning towards the

6

shed. Me shouting crazy "Bugger off you flamin bitch, bugger off."' He pulled up his pants and asked Vincent the time.

The dog sniffed at Vincent's boots, looked up, his ears all alert. Vincent gave the dog a cursory pat. 'Friendly fellow.'

'Not mine. Belongs to lakeside campers.'

'Oh?'

'They fled on the ship come to evacuate holiday makers stranded here. Pets excluded. I'm minding him for now. Keeps me company, you see.' Damien licked his lips and shoved his facemask into his pocket looking undecided and seemingly still on edge.

Clouds were billowing into mushrooms over the lake. He frowned pointing to it.

'See that? Not clouds, mate, but bloody smoke. I tell yeh there's fires still out there. Across the lake.'

It looked more like clouds to Vincent, but he didn't wish to interrupt or contradict.

'The wind's the culprit. Gets it going.' Damien felt his clean-shaven chin with his good hand, but his gaze was on his ash-covered boots and his thoughts elsewhere.

'I tell yeh, mate,' said Damien his voice full of foreboding, 'This here fire's not done. Not by a long shot. You see it popping up all over the bloody country. Not like Black Saturday or Ruby Tuesday, or whatever. It's different, mate. Quite something else. Armageddon's the word in the papers. Them politicians need to take note.' He breathed heavily and broke into a fit of coughing.

~

They both sat in stillness waiting for the physiotherapist to turn up. The wind swirled around them once more and then seemed to die. The haze dissipated like morning smog, and patches of sky were visible over the lake. Just then the physio lady turned up.

'You waiting to see me? she asked, her motherly eyes on Damien's swollen hand. 'Come in, love.'

'I'll be around, Damien. We'll talk more after you're done.'

'Much appreciate you giving me a ear and all that,' said Damien as he secured the leash to the leg of the bench on which they had sat. The spaniel whimpered once and curled up under the bench. 'He'll be right,' said Damien over his shoulders as he disappeared into the Hub.

~

Vincent was about to turn and head back in to join his team when a woman appeared from the car park around the corner.

'Almost sure that's Damien I spotted just then,' she said stepping right up to Vincent.

'You know him?'

'Yep, he's with Doug, my husband in the Men's Shed.' She appeared to have come in somewhat of a hurry – ruffled blonde hair with strands of grey, crumpled floral top with sleeves just below elbow, knee-length cotton pants and sandals. She rested her Coles shopping bag at her feet and blew her nose in a tissue. Eyes weepy.

Vincent gave her a concerned look.

'No, I'm not crying. Just hay fever,' she explained. 'Come for the GROCON meeting. Am I late?'

'Sorry but that was yesterday at 5. Not sure of another meeting today.'

The woman bit her lip and looked away with troubled eyes.

'I'll find out for you,' said Vincent. 'But can I first get you a cuppa?'

'Dear me, counted on some help today. Husband's not up to it. Bit crook, you see. Our sheds and fencing went down with the fire. Told not to clean up, not to touch things. Asbestos and stuff, you know.'

'That's not good.' Vincent sounded sympathetic. 'Relax a minute and I'll fetch you that hot drink,'

'Thanks,' said the lady 'I could do with a cuppa. All nerves, you see. My husband isn't up to it today,' she repeated. 'Have to get him to the doctor.' She rummaged in her shopping bag for more tissues.

Eve, Vincent's team leader, soon arrived with the tea, introduced herself and sat close to the lady. She said her name was Judy and that a kind Red Cross man had offered to get her some information. Vincent presently emerged and handed Judy a piece of paper.

'As I thought, there's no meeting today. I phoned GROCON. They've set themselves up in the building next to the pub in the main street. You know the one. A man called Steve, he'll see you, answer all your questions and get you going.'

Judy sighed, perceptibly dropping her shoulders. 'My daughter's in Melbourne. Says it's up to me to keep strong. But it's just too hard, you know. Nursing me Doug and keeping healthy. Just too hard. Now *this* had to happen.'

'So sorry about the difficult time you're having,' said Eve, taking the empty cup from Judy.

'But we're doing good,' Judy said with a feeble smile. 'Have to be positive, you know. We're lucky. Not like some others. Poor Damien lost his home, all of it. Was helping his neighbour, I heard.'

Vincent, standing before the two seated women scanning his phone, looked up startled. Poor bugger, he thought.

'You both live in the same street then?' he said.

'No, no. I'm in Terra Nova Drive. He's in Bastion Point Road. Both streets badly hit. Like Chinese dragons had come by breathing fire.'

'But your house - what happened?'

'Don't ask me, dear. A miracle it's still standing – apart from the shed, of course.'

'And you were stuck there, in the open?' said Eve wide-eyed.

'Oh god, no. Husband and I and me near neighbours with littlies didn't chance it. We got driven by the cops to the lake just as the fires threatened. Heaps of holiday makers, kids included, couldn't get out. We huddled together, fearing the worst? Mind you, it still keeps me awake, what with the howling wind and the night sky on fire. Lit up all our faces, it did. Like ghost lanterns.'

Eve put her arm around Judy. Vincent had some personal sense of her terror. Even so, he couldn't imagine what it must have been like to be stranded at night in knee deep water, with a fast- approaching fire front.

Judy jumped up, grabbing her shopping bag 'But I'd better be going,' she said wiping her runny eyes. 'Hubby must be fretting. Say *hi* to Damien for me. He could do with some sympathy.'

Vincent and Eve stretched their legs by taking a short stroll past the Men's Shed to the very edge of the fire ravaged bush. A well-used walking trail was visible through the bush, but it was cordoned off with a length of yellow duct tape with the words *Danger Keep Out* in red.

Vincent was pleased that he'd hardly noticed how the morning had slipped by. Good so far, he thought. However, the weather continued to be a bother. Sultry one minute and chilly the next. Just then there were a few droplets of rain, and now sunshine. He was aware that some town folks were troubled that heavy rains may wash toxic ash from burnt homes and sheds into the lake.

'I've made you ham and cheese sandwiches,' said Vincent as Damien came out after his physiotherapy. It was wrapped haphazardly in sheets of paper towel. Damien sat immediately and took large bites, his eyes fixed on it. The spaniel wagged his tail in furious expectation.

'Was it helpful - the physiotherapy, I mean?'

'She couldn't do much. *Inflamed* was her exact word.' He fed the dog with the crusts he'd saved, wiping his mouth with the back of his good hand. 'Insisted I see my doctor today.'

'Yes, that's sensible advice,'

Vincent was keen to get Damien speaking about how he was handling his loss. There'd likely be something he could learn about coping better. But how to broach the subject as Damien was about to set off for the doctor's.

'A woman came by earlier. Calls herself Judy. Said to say *hi* to you. Oh, and she told us that two streets in town had it really bad, houses totally wiped out. Yeah, I'm keen to see the destruction for myself. May drive there later.' He pulled out an A-4 size map of the town neatly folded and tucked in the back pocket of his pants. 'Can you please point me to the streets, Damien?'

'No need for that. I'll take you to Bastion Point Road myself. That's my street'

'Would you?' That's great,' said Vincent his eagerness and appreciation all too visible. 'I'll ask my team if anyone wants to join us. We'll take the Red Cross station wagon. But you get to your doctor first. I'll wait.'

'Right.' Damien bent down to untether his spaniel from the bench. 'Suppose Judy filled you in on how it went with me?' said Damien with a barely suppressed tremor in his voice.

'Yeah, it shattered us to know your house burnt down while you were helping your neighbour. Simply awful, mate. Wish there's something we could do to help.' Vincent felt the feebleness of his sympathy in proportion to Damien's loss. He wished he could re-live Damien's nightmare, take on his pain. It triggered once more his memory of that fateful Black Saturday in 2009 trapped on that oval in Marysville with his wife. In that dire moment Dante's *Inferno* had come to mind. But why this urge to see Damien's flattened house and re-live his anguish? Self-indulgence or perversity? But maybe, just maybe, it could spur him to move on. Finally. Who can tell for sure?

~

Late that afternoon, he drove Damien to his gutted property. The spaniel was left in the Ute with a handful of pellets and

12

a firm 'Stay!' Eve joined them. They parked at the entrance into Bastion Point Road and walked to give them a feeling of immediacy. Damien went a few paces ahead. It was a grim site.

'Here, this is it,' he said in a voice seemingly devoid of emotion. 'People fled right away when the police came - missus and my boy Roan included. Not me. Stubborn like.'

'Don't tell me you hoped to stand your ground and save all these houses?' said Vincent in disbelief as his eyes took in the heaps of rubble and twisted metal on both sides of Bastion Point Road as far as was visible, with an occasional chimney standing erect and abandoned. Eve simply stared with her hand cupped to her mouth. Almost every house in the street was charred, flattened and no longer recognizable as once lived-in sanctuaries for joyful families. 'It's like barrel-bombed houses,' whispered Eve, not wanting Damien to hear her. She looked pale.

A thicket of scorched and stripped eucalyptus behind the line of flattened properties stood gaunt against the late afternoon sky. A magpie flew past in an undecided manoeuvre. Frail tree limbs were rattled by the breeze. Shells of two gutted vehicles stood bereft on bare rims.

Damien nodded to where his house once stood. 'Gave the roof and walls a good drenching. My mates were out with their hoses and sprinklers. Puffs of smoke and got me gasping. Heard fierce cracking away somewhere whipped up by the wind.' He went still for a moment staring at his boots sorely needing attention. 'Yeah, I felt unnerved by how dark it got. Christ, only two in the afternoon.'

It's late afternoon now thought Vincent, and things are

still brightly visible, but eerily bright.

'The fire stormed in like bunched rally-cars,' continued Damien, 'took the trees, shook them good like with flaming hands.' He seemed pressured now to tell it all. He removed his glasses with his crook hand, as if his eyes wild and bloodshot needed cooling. Vincent held out his compact tissue pack, but he looked away.

'Take it easy, Damien,' urged Eve offering him her water bottle. 'Let's take a breather. But Damien wouldn't be persuaded otherwise. He leaned against the station wagon and soothed his bandaged hand. 'Yeah man,' he continued 'everything went hellish crazy. Bloody sparks biting into me arms and face, embers large as my foot landing on houses. Peter's roof took fire. Fuck, fuck I shouted running about, tugging at my hose, hoping to lend a hand.'

How unreal, mused Vincent, this firestorm was no less hellish than what had hit him and others in Marysville. He hadn't considered then that such a thing would repeat itself, at another time and place. But now....

'A gas bottle exploded across over there in the garage on the other side,' continued Damien. 'More boom, boom followed. One house after another went down.' He paused, coughed, and looked at the others, his eyes glazing over. 'But see,' he said as an afterthought, 'Peter's house still stands – but not mine. And me Betsy, she's gone too. For good.'

'How's that?' said Vincent taken aback.

Eve stiffened and caught her colleague's eye. Betsy? Had she not been attentive to Damien's story?

It was a long minute, before Damien found his voice again. 'I tried to shove her into the car with my wife, but me

German Shepherd was stubborn like me. Stuck to me from when I picked her up at the lake. Running about like crazy when I spotted her. Dumped by some drunken lout, I guess, a camper likely. Ten years that'd be. Yeh, Betsy become a crook old lady since. Couldn't take firecrackers and the like. Dog nerves, I guess.' He slumped into a squat, picked up a partially burnt twig and scratched the ground in ferocious motion. The twig snapped.

Vincent and Eve stood tongue-tied, their discomfort telling. A vague smell of burnt toast drifted in the air. Real or imagined, Vincent couldn't tell.

'Hadn't paid her much attention, you see,' said Damien in a spent voice. He sniffled and stood up with a sigh. 'I whistled and shouted, called her name. Jesus, she just never turned up.' He removed his misted-over glasses and blinked in the sunlight. 'Blokes dream nightmares. Here was it, mate – the real devil dancing in the fire.'

~

There was little more to his story other than that they were rescued by a fire truck which turned up belatedly. Vincent and Eve wondered what had become of the German Shepherd. How did she perish in the fire? Perhaps too painful a question to ask now. Vincent had never been a pet lover and couldn't quite make sense of why some people attach to dogs as if they were kids – grieve hugely when a dog died or had to be put down. Quite silly really. But then he recalled how hurt he felt when his neighbour friend hinted that it was foolish to grieve over a *potential* child that wasn't exactly born. Just a stillbirth, mate, he'd said, so enraging Vincent that he swore blue murder, frightening the pants off his friend.

Just then Eve drew their attention to a police car heading down Bastion Point Road, slow and deliberate. The officer got out, hitched up his black pants, surveying the group. Perhaps making sure they weren't outsiders come thieving.

'You know this street is off-limits for now?'

Vincent raised his eyebrows. They were told each property had to be cleared of toxic ash contamination by the EPA.

'Sorry Officer,' said Vincent 'it's my fault. I asked Damien to bring us here. We're just about to push off'.

~

Eve sat in the back of the car with Damien giving him company as Vincent drove.

'If you don't mind, I'll get my car and get going,' said Damien. 'Need to rest this hand.' It was almost as if the painful throbbing had been forgotten, temporarily, while he was recounting his ordeal. But now it had returned with a vengeance.

'Yes, do that,' said Eve. 'But where's your family sheltering?'

'We're a charity case for now,' said Damien sounding not at all pleased about it.

'Pretty much living on handouts. Good wife managed to get some financial help from the government. Disaster Relief, I think she said. So, we're housed for now at the Beachcomber Caravan Park. Yeah, and this shirt and pants I picked up at the Salvos.'

'Yeah, I noticed it's a fashionable pair of jeans you got on there,' said Vincent catching Damien's eye in the rear-view mirror. 'Holes and frays in all the right places, and the belt a contrasting shade of brown.'

That got Damien laughing. They joined in.

~

As they were getting out of the Red Cross vehicle at the Health Hub, Eve spotted two of her colleagues across the road excitedly gazing up at a tall gum, almost stripped of life by the recent inferno. They were pointing at something like a large ball stuck high up at the crotch of two branches. A young man on a bicycle had stopped and joined them.

'What's up?' shouted Eve.

'Come. Come see. We spotted a koala with a cute baby on its back.' Eve rushed over to see for herself.

Got to be a miracle, thought Vincent as he walked Damien to his car and waited to see him off. The spaniel, shut in the car, went wild with excitement.

'What you think of that, Damien, a mother koala with its joey survived the fires?'

Damien hesitated before getting into his car, looked up at the lump high in the branches of the partially burnt gum now sprouting feeble new growth. 'It's all good, mate, all good.' The spaniel, adopted for now, licked the back of Damien's neck with joy. Damien's eyes softened.

At that moment, Vincent saw the earnest face of Anna, her words carried to him in the breeze.

House Auctions

'Yeah, that's it, Hashim. It's how houses are sold here. Auctioned,' Auntie Jay said.

'Really?'

On our arrival in Australia in 1988, we lived in Elsternwick with a relative of my wife's, Auntie Jay, also an ex-South African. A gesture of temporary goodwill. Most migrants need a leg-up to make it in a new country.

Auctions are a nightmare for new migrants. It certainly was for my wife and me when we went house hunting thirty years ago. In my experience, houses were always advertised in the papers under the *Properties for Sale* columns. At least this was how it was done in South Africa. We'd never experienced auctions until we set foot here.

'In fact, two houses in our street are up for auction in a fortnight. You must have seen the auction boards.'

'No, haven't paid much attention. Jet lag and all that.'

'But surely you can't not have seen them. Large, and almost in your face with airbrushed photos of the property.'

Auntie Jay was eager to help. And for our part, we did not wish to overstretch her hospitality.

'I'll take you both to the auctions. But you'll be interested to see the houses before then when they're open for inspection.'

'Eh?'

Auntie Jay explained how in the weeks before the auction, houses were prepared for inspection to prospective buyers.

In two months, we'd made some progress settling in. My wife was already in a reasonably well-paying job, and I'd lined up a few promising interviews. It was time to take on the next challenge: buying a house.

Having already attended a few auctions, we now had some idea of how it worked. But we still lacked confidence. Even visualizing ourselves out there actually bidding was enough to give me the jitters. Auntie Jay coaxed us with a reassuring step-by-step strategy – first scan the auction pages in the Friday issue of the *Melbourne Age,* highlight a few houses in Ormond, Bentleigh, and Glen Huntly - suburbs close to family support. And then check them out before the auction.

'Oh thanks. That certainly helps. Is that it?'

'No, no. You'll have to work out how big a house will suit you – bedrooms, garage, single or double storey, big or small back yard. You know, things like that. But also, what you can afford.'

'My god, it's now getting complicated,' sighed my wife, draining the last drop from her water bottle.

'And that's not all,' continued Auntie Jay like she relished inflicting pain. 'Houses away from high traffic roads, closer to parks, schools, shops and public transport cost more. Much more. Even beyond what the bank may loan you.'

~

We had a few sleepless nights before fronting up to bid for the first house that struck our fancy and had passed our *tick-box* test.

'Look at the kitchen, dear. Clean and neat. Even has a dish washer. You do know domestic help is unheard of here. Not like in Durban.'

'Not so loud, Deb.' I whispered, a little sensitive to prospective buyers nearby, opening and closing cupboards.

~

I recall us elbowing past a throng of people in the passageway, just before the auction was to commence. It had three smallish bedrooms, two with built in wardrobes, plus a new kitchen. What's more, it was near a train station and a respectable shopping strip. What else would we need?

'But wait,' Auntie Jay said, all starry eyed. 'Just think, you'll be a stone's throw from Chaddy.'

'Chaddy, what's Chaddy?'

'Oops sorry. Forgot you're new here.'

'Well?'

'Chadstone is a mega shopping complex. Some say largest in the Southern Hemisphere.'

'Wow, Hashim, then we must get this house,' my wife said with a determined look.

Yeah, at all costs, I thought.

~

Presently we were all ushered to the front of the house for the auction. Fortunately, the sun was out. It was warm and cheerful. The crowd closed in and faced the auctioneer, a jaunty man of about 40 full of himself; slick from head to toe

- clean-cut face, plastered hair, dark suit, red tie, and shiny pointy shoes. Black. I thought it interesting how estate agents, politicians, financial planners, and insurance brokers seem to be made from the same mould – a fast-talking class of their own.

People stood all over the place, on the pavements and nature-strips – men and women, a few kids, a passive black Labrador next to a wriggling child in a pram. Everyone seemed expectant yet a little nervous, shifting on their feet and looking away from the auctioneer, who had a rolled-up wad of paper in his right hand. He scanned the crowd with a practised eye before rattling off the rules of the auction, and then highlighting the assets of the property on offer.

In the meantime, two of his team moved among the crowd. They showed particular interest in two Asian couples who had turned up. Once the auction was in progress, the agents seemed to egg them to stay ahead of other bids. I found this quite annoying.

It was not surprising then that we lost this house, even without raising a finger. It sold for what we thought was a preposterous sum. So, you would guess how devastated we felt when the possibility of owning this house also popped like a bubble as the auctioneer struck the rolled-up paper for a third and decisive time. Within minutes, the chatting crowd shifted and dispersed leaving us stranded and wondering what next. A middle-aged woman with a gaudy perm, fancy sunglasses and a bulging Emilio Masi bag disappeared into the house with the auctioneer.

~

Gloom and despair took over. The little confidence we had,

evaporated. We couldn't imagine ourselves ever winning in this mindless auction game. But we soldiered on.

Here I am now years later often driving past that dream house that we lost and resisting an urge to pull over and inspect it - yet again. I smile wryly. How ironic that I should now feel convinced it would have been an absolutely bad buy. How perceptions shift with time and circumstances! The truth is that desperation to own a house had blunted our judgement then. How could we have even considered this property a good enough option?

I marvel at how hideous it looks, squatting there like a bullfrog, partially hidden behind a couple of gums. The front yard is narrow and neglected. Four pillars support the front gable over an L-shaped veranda, pillars that remind me of the stumpy legs of a hippo. Yes, that's it, a squatting bullfrog with ungainly hippo legs. How bizarre! Moreover, it is a weather board house, over fifty years old I'd say, on noisy Glen Huntly Road. The colours of the exterior walls are revolting– industrial green in the veranda, and the rest of the walls a shitty ochre. Oh well, there's no accounting for people's tastes.

~

September slipped by taking its cue from July and August. I was still without a job. Auntie Jay made as if caught in much business, hence leaving us with the burden of finding a place to live. Perhaps she'd be thinking: 'I did my bit showing them the ropes. It's up to them now how they sort themselves out.' Apart from casually mentioning one day that she was expecting visitors from South Africa over Christmas, she rarely now enquired what luck we were having in house hunting. The atmosphere had become decidedly cool. We felt the pressure and regretted migrating to Australia.

There was no turning back now. The only option was to keep at it. The *Sunday Age* usually listed the houses auctioned and sold on the previous day, or passed in. I was beginning to understand how the housing market worked. We also routinely checked the *Houses for sale and auction* columns in this edition. The listings were generally sparse when compared with that in the Friday's *Age* newspaper.

On the second Sunday of November, we decided to check out a house in Hughesdale. It was open for inspection and was to be auctioned in a fortnight's time. When borrowing Auntie Jay's car, we mentioned that we were headed to inspect a property in Hughesdale.

'But why so far?' she queried.

'Oh, we heard the houses there were more affordable,' I explained wondering why she thought it was too far.

In any case, we drove slowly up Darling Street looking for the house in question. Paperbark trees lined the nature strip on either side of the street. Not too many cars parked along the kerb. I pulled up beside the *For Auction* board on my side.

'No that can't be right,' said my wife who had the *Age* in her hand and was reading off the street numbers. 'It says No. 17 Darling Street. But we've stopped at No. 11.'

I glanced at the newspaper. 'Yeah, No. 11's not even listed. That's strange.'

We got out and stood scanning the noticeboard. Then took

in the property. The house was a 1950s weatherboard, in reasonably good condition – at least on the outside. Nothing fancy. A jacaranda tree with an expansive canopy graced the front garden. Sitting underneath on a well-tended lawn was a wheelbarrow converted to a flowerbox, now overflowing with pink and purple petunias in full bloom. A single white butterfly flitted about. Along the perimeters of the garden were upright wooden trellises which supported sweet peas, in a riot of colours. What an impressive show on a bright summer's day!

'You interested in our house?' It was an elderly woman who appeared from the side of the building, with a green watering can. A small energetic woman with an apron over a loose floral dress, floppy hat, runners, and garden gloves. She smiled and the creases of her aged face reflected her delight.

'Sorry,' I said, feeling a little flustered.' No, no, just looking. Hope it's, okay?'

'Will be in the papers next Saturday.'

'Oh, thanks,' added Deb. 'That explains it.'

The lady put down her can and removed her hat revealing a dishevelled white fluff.

She wiped her brow on the sleeve of her overall. 'Predict a scorcher today,' she said taking a step towards us, a knee-height picket fence separating us.

'Where you from – India? All us folks in this street born Aussies. Mostly built our own houses.'

A warm breeze stirred in the jacaranda.

'When'll your house be open for inspection?' queried Deb.

'Oh, you could come in now if you wish. Meet Mal my

husband. He'll be keen to show you the place.'

I glanced at my wife to see if she was as taken aback as I was with the spontaneous invitation.

'Thanks, but we don't wish to intrude on your privacy. Especially on a Sunday,' said Deb.

'No, no, no worries. Give me a sec while I open the gate. Come in and I'll get something to cool you down. Mind the sun. Simply bad, you know.'

The house felt much cooler inside than outside. With windows shuttered and curtains drawn, the dim lighting seemed to add to the cooling effect.

An elderly man with a smooth cheerful face and a comfortable paunch waddled into the living room, bare feet, singlet, and black track pants. His thinning hair was plastered back, adding to his broad forehead.

'Hello, hello and who have we here, Marge?'

'Folks looking for a house. Show them around, dear.'

Marge apologised for not introducing herself earlier. We told them our names and a little of who we were. While Marge got us drinks, Mal painted us a picture of his life story which it appeared was tied up intimately with this house and his long marriage to Marge. He pointed to photos on the shelf above the fireplace saying his two daughters were born here and have since grown into adults and set themselves up in life. No grandchildren as yet. 'But' he added with a wistful look, 'one can't have everything in life.'

In half an hour, Deb and I felt strangely at home, as if we belonged to this house. Marge and Mal had so warmed to us, that they seemed quite in earnest to entrust their house to us, the place in which they had invested almost their entire adult lives.

They pointed out things they'd leave behind for the new owners, items they'd not need or accommodate in their one-room unit at Happy Valley Retirement Village. The items included a wall unit with a selection of drink glasses, a kitchen table and chairs, garden furniture, and two well-used cane chairs installed side-by-side in the fernery, with a panoramic view of a thriving back garden. Marge explained they'd especially miss the chairs because this was where they'd sat with their breakfast, lunch, and dinners all through many, many summers. Such a loss. 'But not to worry', she said with a laugh. They'd not be leaving behind their memories for the next occupants. That would be giving away far too much.

~

So it was that we came to live at 11 Darling Street, Hughesdale, thirty years ago. The house was withdrawn from auction and sold to us at a bargain basement price. Auntie Jay fell off her chair when told.

'Your colour didn't matter to them? That's truly remarkable.'

~

We kept in touch with both Mal and Marge until the very end. *They knew where they were going, smiling at death in the shade of a ghost-gum. (Bruce Chatwin: The Songlines.)*

Toilet Stories

'It must be an aisle seat and close to the toilets,' I tell the travel agent.

Lavatory that's what I look for on my Qantas flight. I like the earthy frankness of the sound. It oozes everything natural. When I'm on holiday in a foreign country and am desperate for a pee, helpful strangers point me to a toilette, washroom, bathroom, restroom, or powder room. This is annoying. Why? Because I'm not for a posh place which expects a fee for a pee.

But then a *closet* is not for me either as I'd imagine it would be too claustrophobic. However, I don't mind a *latrine* or a *loo* as these are as good as a lavatory. Come to think of it, a *dunny* outshines any *shithouse* if you ask me. Invariably located at the bottom of a weedy back yard, the dunny asserts itself in a natural setting, cobwebs, and all. Here one can *crap* feeling quite liberated, without inhibitions or fear of eavesdroppers stealing your thunder. What with bloated flies keeping you company and steam rising from the depths to caress your bottom, you're certain to enjoy a rare sense of release.

~

'Don't ever try the new-fangled automated toilet at South Bank,' said the first young woman creasing her brow. 'It's a tease, if not a challenge.'

Two women clad in office-style black outfits were waiting, as I was, at Flinders Street station for the 6 pm Oakleigh train.

'Really,' said her companion.

'Yeh, desperate or not, you'd be kept waiting. Some invisible eye scans you before the door opens to let you in.'

'Go'n.'

'Even then you can't rush in and squat. No, no. The door takes its own sweet time to slide shut while you cramp your thighs to prevent a leak.'

'How awful,' said the second woman looking bemused and incredulous. The first woman buttoning her winter coat, glanced in the direction of the soon to arrive train.

The crowd was building up and an anxious few moved in front of me. Drawn to their conversation, I edged a discreet distance from the ladies - not wanting to miss a potential writing theme. The first women continued undeterred that our train was announced to arrive in two minutes.

'I'm about to squat with knickers at my knee when I notice a flickering red light with the instruction *Lock the door*. Oh my god, I jump to it.'

'You're joking, aren't you?'

'Imagine if I hadn't seen it. The door could have slid open, and there I'd be in the midst of a steady pee!'

A snort and laugh attract the puzzled attention of people nearby.

'Come on Kate. It's your imagination's taking off again.'

'No laughing matter, I tell you. I'd have been mortified to death if the intruder turned out to be a cute guy.'

The train arrives. People alight, while others on the platform push and shove past and clog the entrance. 'Excuse me, excuse me please,' I urge as I pry a passage to the inner aisle of the coach and grab the overhead rail as the train lurches forward. What do you know, my two young women have found seats just where I stood – facing each other. They sat silent for a long while. My thoughts took me elsewhere.

'No, there's no liberal supply of toilet paper. Not in this toilet,' said lady number one determined to complete her story.

A half-interested smile from her companion followed by a stifled yawn.

'At each press of a button, just two flimsy sheets rationed by the dispenser. If you tug hoping for more, the bloody sheet breaks into bits. This is just too much, I say, and hasten to clean up. Just then a sweet music fills the cubicle, and a gentle reassuring voice announces, "You still have 45 second left, thank you."'

~

Some days later I relate this story over drinks with my wife and her squash friends – embellishing it suitably for greater hilarity. It elicits much laughter. This triggers a few more toilet stories. Luanne says with a giggle and a nudge of her husband Benny:

'Remember how you found yourself shut in one of these automatic loos in London and the light went out, and the automatic cleaning mode came on?'

'Yeah, of course. The fright I got. Shit, shit, shit I

screamed and banged the door to be let out.'

'He was ashamed, miserable and very much feeling like a rain-soaked rooster.'

'And very angry,' added Benny. 'I'll sue the buggers,' I shouted attracting a crowd of amused sympathizers. 'I never did, but rather slunk off to the hotel to change and recover.'

'And have a much-needed pee,' said Luanne.

Grave New World

'Hey, don't shout, I can't hear you. Slow down, would ye.'

Ha, that's certainly Bianna. Who's she annoyed with now? Seems on the phone. I throw off the bedcover and get up in one determined motion. It's near ten by the wall clock. I feel a little unsteady, despite eleven hours of sleep. Been this way since a Covid-like flu hit me a week ago. Tested negative, as if that means anything. I make my way downstairs, gingerly holding onto the rail. Barefoot. Bianna's whacking the pots in the sink.

'Hello dear,' I say sweetly and go over and peck her on the nape of her neck. She doesn't turn around. 'Who was on the phone just then?'

'My shitty son, of course. Who else?' She wipes her hands brusquely on her apron and glares as if I'm to blame. 'Ashbo skipped uni classes. Second time this week. He wants to be an authentic *black* man, he says. To prove it, he's in the thick of a BLM protest.'

'You mean there's a Black Lives Matter thing happening here in Bristol? Good lord, it's the ghost of George Floyd come to shake a fist at Colston.'

'I wish you'd be serious for once, Paul.'

Yes, I should temper my flippant habit, I think. I dish myself a helping of stewed apple cooked the evening before and plonk myself on a high stool at the kitchen counter. 'Shall I make you some toast, dear?' No response. Couldn't tell what Bianna feels about the protest.

'He phoned to ask me to join them. Not to miss history in the making,' he said. 'Students mobilising the local folks and holiday visitors.'

'That should be some fun, love. Shall we?' I stick my bowl in the sink and start on the toast, making an extra slice for Bianna – just in case. I gaze out of the window. About time I tried some other way to get onto the good side of Ashbo, I think. He's so oppositional since I moved in with his mother, usurping their cosy closeness. He's been moody and sullen says Bianna, since she and her husband split. Out of loyalty to his dad, I guess. He insists on calling me a *whitey.* Hurtful, but I have to live with it as best as possible.

'Hey, watch the toast!'

I rush to turn on the extractor fan as the smell of burnt toast fills the air.

'Be more careful, dear, or you'll burn down the house one day.'

~

Bianna joins me over coffee and toast. We talk about the demonstration down at the Avon riverfront.

'You shouldn't be going out Paul, not just yet. The doctor said so. Look at you. Like the last man out of Auschwitz.'

'That's a hilarious image.' I laugh. 'Surely, I don't look like a Bristol scarecrow!'

She grins. 'But you do worry me, love. At seventy, you

need to take better care of yourself.'

I find the slave history of Bristol unpleasant thinking about. Mostly skirt around it. But it's never too far from my awareness. Glaring landmarks all over the city to needle me. Like a nasty smell leaching from hidden drains. On school excursions to the docks and the maritime museum, we learned of Edward Colston, a wealthy maritime trader and owner of tall sailing ships who earned enormous riches for the citizens of Bristol. We stood at the foot of the man's statue in harsh sunlight and squinted to catch a glimpse of his large bronze face, his uncut locks falling onto his shoulders. Our great-grandfather's wealth, we were reminded, flowed generously through the veins of his descendants – me included. The truth did get to me in drips over time. Colston traded in slaves, buying and selling African men, women and children.

'I suppose with my Caribbean roots, the BLM movement should matter to me, Paul. But I really don't know if I can take the pushing and shoving by rowdy crowds,' says Bianna, buttering her toast. 'Makes me nervous. Wouldn't wish to catch this fearful virus.'

'You decide, love. I'm easy.' I go around and hug her.

'Ashbo's troublesome. He'll feel peeved if I don't turn up.'

I could tell she was feeling quite conflicted.

We're an odd couple. It's a fact. She's short, chocolate-brown, broad-nosed, frizzy hair and an earnest disposition. Me, pale-skinned, a Greek nose, lanky, shocking unruly hair, a set grin, and mostly irreverent. But her people and my people are bound by a grim historical reality. My ancestors traded her African ancestors to the slave colonies in the

Caribbean as plantation labour.

'So, love, what you say?' I tog myself warmly and we walk to the ridge overlooking the Harbour Boulevard to get a sight of the protest. At least then Ashbo may tolerate me in the house. Who knows, he may still be sufficiently fired up at dinner tonight and speak about his experience of the day.

The summer light streamed into the kitchen, catching Bianna in a glow as she drained her coffee and handed me the cup. My turn to do the dishes. Reluctant or not, I usually got my way with Bianna. Today, I eventually won her over with one of my contrived jokes – *Why does Mr Monkey cross the road? Answer: His monkey business is on the other side!*

'That's absolutely stupid, Paul.' She laughed. 'You always embarrass me in company with such rubbish. But others seem to love it. Beats me every time. Okay, now go get changed. And leave the dressing gown you have on in the laundry. And about time.'

~

I stood momentarily on the back step, waiting for Bianna. The ungated dirt yard opening onto Raleigh Street just beyond was shaded by old pine trees. Two cars parked to the one side. When she finally emerged, Bianna *tick-boxed* me to ensure I was all set. Hat, mask, sanitiser, water, medication, binoculars, phone. She carried a small pack of cut fruit.

'No more than ninety minutes, right?' she instructed. 'Shouldn't miss your afternoon nap, dear. And remember *social distancing.*'

'Yes Sarge.' I saluted. 'Righto!'

Just down the street, we ran into energetic Evelyn, our neighbour from a few houses down, returning from walking her frisky spaniel. She had company. Her face lit up in surprise when told we were headed to the BLM protest.

'Oh, that sounds exciting. Can we go along? Sorry, this is Matt, by the way, my cousin, on a business trip from Melbourne.'

'Sure thing, why not,' I said. 'The more the merrier.'

She disappeared into her house to settle her dog while we chatted with Matt. He was a portly man in his fifties, with a ruddy face and an almost bald head.

'There's been some disruption to my flights, else I'd have been home a few days ago. Funny thing that I'm now to see a BLM protest here in Bristol when my wife told me only last night of similar big marches in Melbourne and elsewhere.'

I stepped aside to let a large woman pass by with a pram. We all spontaneously sneaked a peak. The baby was blissfully asleep. We smiled.

'That's right,' said Bianna adjusting her facemask, 'I caught a bit of it on the morning news. Protests about the ongoing detention of indigenous peoples, it said. Including kids as young as ten. Unbelievable. The police were rather active in discouraging the march taking place, apparently charging organisers.'

'Yeah, the government's not happy.' Matt frowned. 'They're in a bind with the pandemic not letting up.'

Just then Evelyn turned up, striding briskly. She had on a wide-brimmed floral hat, fresh lipstick, and sunglasses. Bianna raised her eyebrows. We set off down the road that led generally in the direction of the waterfront, hoping to catch the protest march somewhere in the vicinity. It was a question of trusting our noses to get us there.

~

As we turned into Burtle Road, we were rather surprised to see many people ahead, perhaps with the same intention as us. I noticed Matt's interest in the buildings here, old, and care-worn, but still bravely standing up to some modest restoration and use, low-rental shops mostly.

'Remind me later, Matt, to tell you about the graffiti all along here, especially about the illusive artist, Banksy.'

Intrigued, Matt nodded. Burtle Road was cobbled and relatively narrow, and the pavement even narrower. Unbroken lines of parked vehicles at either kerb compelled us to take to the middle of the road. Fortunately, not much traffic troubled us which I thought was unusual. The women set the pace. Bianna was never happy going on a walk with me as I seldom kept up, which frustrated her no end.

'You have to get your heart pumping,' she always insisted.

~

When we got to the steepest point in the road overlooking the docks, I suggested we stop for coffee at the High Point Café, which had seating on the second-level balcony. My suggestion was quite brilliant, I thought, since we'd have an expansive view. In fact, from across the road, we spotted a clutch of patrons on the balcony, standing and gesticulating towards the waterfront. Faint rallying cries drifted our way.

'No dear,' protested Bianna, 'we don't have time for coffee.'

'But why? I thought this was as far as we intended to come to catch a glimpse of the demonstration. The balcony is the best vantage point.'

Matt looked a little uncomfortable and embarrassed.

'I'm sure, love, Matt and Evelyn would like a closer look at the crowd.'

Evelyn murmured in full agreement.

It's annoying how Bianna tended to change her mind. I felt my jaw tighten. And what's more, my facemask wasn't helping matters.

'Okay then, if you say so. But let's stay close. And if we're separated, let's meet at this café.'

There was visible relief on all three faces. So, we kept going, now with more purpose and haste. But some misgivings remained with me. What if we get sucked into a chaotic throng? What of the pandemic and the safe distance rule?

~

The voices grew ever louder. We turned a corner and found ourselves in College Green, and there ahead of us was a milling crowd of protesters, mostly animated college students by my assessment. They held up placards of all sizes and wordings: *Black Lives Matter*; *White Silence is violence*; *Stop killing us*; *Fuck face masks – I can't breathe*; *Fight modern day slavery*; *Remember the Uighurs*. I couldn't quite make sense of the one that said *Shut this crap down*.

Evelyn scanned the restive crowd. 'We certainly look like a bunch of fuddy-duddies,' she concluded with a look of amusement.

Bianna chortled, adjusting her facemask yet again. 'No hope of finding my son in this melee.'

We fell silent for a moment, wondering 'what next?' I felt uncertain to venture any closer. While many protesters wore masks, even from where I stood, I could tell several didn't. But then, neither Matt nor Evelyn came protected.

~

Obviously responding to some signal, the protesters began moving down Colston Avenue, shouting slogans, and responding in unison to the rallying call: *No justice ... No peace. No justice .... No peace.*

'Okay, I'll stick around here. You all feel free to join the protest. Go on, then.' Bianna frowned, clearly undecided. In the end we mostly stuck together, trailing at a slow pace. Matt had his phone out busy capturing the rare moment for family back in Australia.

The police in orange vests and masks stood by in large numbers but didn't discourage the march in any visible way. The media, too, were well represented. Microphones on extended arms were thrust into the faces of protesters, seeking their comment. For me the situation was one of chaotic movement and cacophony – quite giddying. To compound matters, the summer sun was at its zenith and the air was still. A weariness crept upon me. I drained my water bottle and plodded on, transferring my backpack to my other shoulder.

~

Bianna was in her element. She certainly got into the spirit of the protest, shouting repeatedly from the rear *'Black Lives Matter!'* in her shrill voice, thrusting her fist into the air. I felt a little embarrassed myself and feared she may want me to emulate her. Not exactly sure if the colour of my skin inhibited me. Or my age. It never struck me before that Bristol was home to such a lot of black people. How many were direct descendants of slaves, I wondered, and how many foreign students.

We had not gone for more than twenty minutes when the throng began slowing down. 'What's up?' asked Matt.

'Don't ask me. Perhaps a pitstop,' I joked, reaching out for Bianna's water bottle.

'Goodness me,' shouted Evelyn, who was tall enough to look over the heads of those in front. 'We've stopped at the Colston statue.'

Exactly right, I thought. Makes sense. The protesters intend to make some sort of dramatic anti-racist statement as a finale. We stood far back gaping as they rapidly formed a cordon around the 17th century statue of Edward Colston.

'Tell me about this guy, Paul', whispered Matt. I told him the little I'd been taught at school, the kosher version which painted Colston as a wealthy shipowner, merchant and trader in slaves and commodities who made Bristol prosperous. Certainly not the infamous stuff Ashbo often spat into my face.

'You're no different from the rest of the imperial white pigs,' he would rage. 'How can you not know? Fuckin' check it out, if you're doubting me.'

He would storm out, dismissing pleas from his mother. Of course, he just hates my guts. Clearly, he's talking rubbish. Eight thousand black people branded, herded onto Colston's ships like live animals. Certainly not that many? Fake news, alright? It didn't take me long, however, to verify the truth of the narrative. I felt ashamed.

I so wished now that I could mend my strained relationship with Ashbo. Poor Bianna finds herself to be the meat in the sandwich.

A forest of mobile phones shot up into the air to capture the moment. The protesters egged a daring few to attack the life-size statue mounted on a ten-feet high pedestal. Two men with aerosol cans were given a leg-up. Bronze was soon sprayed red to the accompanying chants of *Murderer, murderer, die!* More hands joined in. Ropes were thrown to them as they balanced precariously on the ledge of the pedestal. The statue was firmly secured, and several rope ends were flung to folks waiting to grab hold of them. Young men and women began to tug and pull the ends. It alarmed me just speculating on the outcome.

Throngs of spectators in the high-rise office blocks across Colston Avenue leaned out of open windows and balconies. Many shouted encouragements, but a vociferous few hurled abuse. *Vandals! Vandals! You black bastards! Why trash history?*

'Hey, where you're going?' I shouted in alarm as Bianna broke rank.

'Ashbo, Ashbo,' she screamed, pushing her way towards the statue which was already rocking on the pedestal and giving way.

'See, that's him.' Evelyn pointed, almost jumping out of her shoes. 'Bianna's son, the tall black guy on the ledge up there with the afro beard and hair. Yellow top.'

'Jesus, Bianna, come back, Colston's about to fall. Someone stop her, hold her back.' I shouted to no one in particular as I thrust myself forward, pushing bodies aside, reaching out in a frantic effort. But my little Bianna simply disappeared into the roused and surging crowd. My chest heaved, I felt faint with panic and lost focus.

'I think he's spotted his mum,' said Evelyn reassuringly, taking hold of me and handing me her water bottle. I noticed Ashbo scramble off his perch shouting at someone below.

To my great relief, Bianna re-emerged through the crowd propelled by the determined arms of Ashbo.

'Now stick with Paul, you hear,' he urged in a grim voice. 'The fun's over, see, so go back home. All of you.'

I said, 'Hi Ashbo, thanks.' He simply looked away, his bearded face dripping with sweat, eyes large and wild. Blotches of red smeared his yellow top. He swung around and disappeared back into the action.

Bianna sighed, looking woebegone. 'I just wanted my son to know I came. But now he seems annoyed I came.'

I hugged her and commiserated. 'But that's not it, dear. He was simply scared you were about to be smashed by Mr Colston landing on your head.' Evelyn and Matt smiled and made sympathetic sounds.

Just then there were loud alerts from the guys on the pedestal. *Get back ... Get back ... Keep clear, give way. Going, going ...* Fearful cheering and clapping rose into the air. A brazen starling took off from a bush nearby, clutching a greasy McDonald's wrapper. Right there, to our great consternation, Colston, bound and lassoed by ropes, gave up his lofty standing with reluctance, swaying and tilting precariously at first, then leaning into a decided fall.

Whohoooooo went the voices in unison, as people stood on their toes to capture the remarkable descent into ignominy of one of Bristol's long-touted benefactors.

The tuggers dropped their ropes and scattered as the bronze monolith hit the ground with a metallic thud. For a moment we four stood in stunned silence while the protesters cheered and danced in great glee, stomping on the statue. One puny girl even knelt on Colston's neck as her photo was taken.

~

'*How the mighty are fallen,*' I whispered, with a mock solemn face. Bianna gave me a puzzled look and grinned.

The police stood by expressionless.

'No social distancing happening here,' shouted Matt almost into my ear.

I suggested we retreat to the safety of the pavement across

Colston Avenue. 'Should we start walking back? I expect the protesters will soon drift away.' Not only was I starving, but I was beginning to worry that a storm was brewing. A sudden breeze caught a line of plane trees along the avenue in disturbed motion. After a sultry morning, the sky was rapidly turning ominous. Hmm, I thought, the white man's god may have been angered.

'A few more minutes,' pleaded Matt. 'I want a close video of Colston on the ground.'

We left the women chatting and edged closer to the statute resting on its back. A bunch of protesters nearby appeared to be consulting. I was certain to see a 17th century man of fame and fortune in a pose of supreme arrogance or triumph. What a shock then to discover that the sculptor had turned Colston into a heroic, contemplative person - forehead all creased, a face deep in thought and cupped in hand. An image of someone leaning heavily on his staff – almost mimicking Rodin's sculpture of the *Thinker*. For some reason, I felt really angry. What deception! You callous and miserable bugger. Lie there in the dirt, for all I care. No sympathy from me.

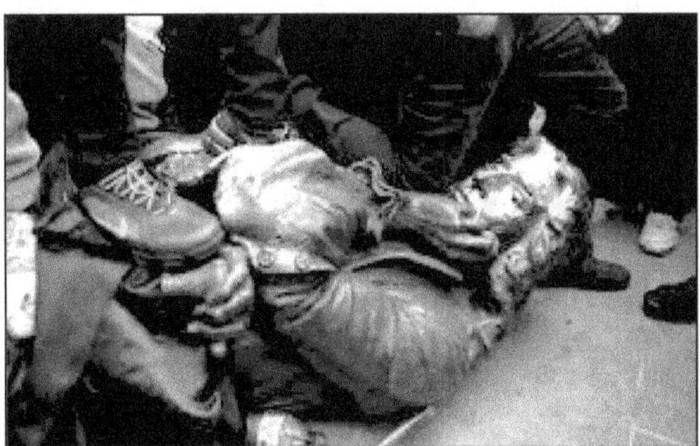

'Hey Paul, look – the women are being interviewed.'

I looked up and noticed that both the cameraman and woman interviewer had *Bristol TV* across the back of their vests. Matt and I rushed across just as Bianna was speaking. I laced my arm in hers for support. She said her son had been in the thick of the protest and that she had Caribbean roots.

'And what about you?' The woman thrust her microphone at Matt, 'As a white Britisher, are you for this BLM protest?'

'I'm Australian actually, here visiting. My wife was in a similar rally in Melbourne only the other night.'

That seemed to grab the interest of the interviewer.

'Was it also about George Floyd and black Americans?'

Bianna couldn't resist cutting in. 'Haven't you heard of black deaths in custody? And indigenous kids as young as ten in detention?' She frowned.

A little ruffled, the interviewer turned to Evelyn.

'How come few facemasks and little social distancing? Isn't it irresponsible for this rally to happen in the middle of a pandemic?'

Evelyn, caught unawares, appeared startled and almost tongue-tied.

'If not now, when?' shouted a scruffy heavyset black student, elbowing in and simultaneously thrusting his placard into the camera, almost knocking the cameraman off his feet. The next second, he'd vanished. I couldn't stop laughing until our attention was drawn by fresh commotion from where Colston lay defaced and grounded. The TV crew rushed to the spot.

They were moving the statue, rolling it along the ground in the direction of the wharf. Many spectators near us gasped obviously guessing the intention of the protesters.

~

Bristol Harbour was only a few hundred metres from where we stood. We rushed across the road into an open grassed public area, found high ground, and watched the bronze hulk being dragged and rolled with the combined effort of many enthusiastic hands. Again, I noticed police standing witness, one of them with a large camera documenting the event.

For a brief moment, Colston was teased and dangled at the water's edge and then unceremoniously dumped. We heard a mighty splash as the sculpture hit the water. Those leaning over the wharf taking photos, jumped back with a scream, and a spontaneous hurrah rose to heaven.

We set off home in a reflective mood. Matt and I tried keeping up with the women. We spoke little. Guilt and potential consequences of shrugging off Covid-19 surfaced, but I kept my mouth shut.

The evening news on Bristol TV, as expected, carried full coverage of the protest and the dramatic toppling of the Colston statue. I gasped when I saw a shot of the statue-less pedestal. It reminded me of the shock I had on seeing my face for the first time after removing my long-cherished moustache. I felt completely nude. My facial landscape had changed.

Bianna and I waited with anticipation to catch ourselves on TV. It didn't happen. But what caught our attention was an irate local member of parliament questioning why the police had stood by and did nothing. Heads may roll, he added.

Hackles up, Bianna fumed. 'We can't let that happen, can we, Paul?'

'Hang on, love, there's the Chief Constable come on. Let's hear his defence.'

'You'd agree it was a volatile situation,' he said 'People were angry. Intervening or arresting anyone may have provoked a major confrontation. But let's be clear, we don't condone vandalisation of public property. Not in the least.'

Ashbo wasn't home for dinner. Bianna fretted. He surfaced for breakfast two days later. Although greatly relieved, Bianna couldn't help but be terse with him, wanting an explanation. He seemed preoccupied, but he sat with us and nibbled at a piece of toast. He even made passing eye contact with me.

'Mum, got to tell you both something.' Ashbo sounded grave. I'd bet he's in some kind of shit. Watch it, Paul, I cautioned myself, not the time for wisecracks.

'A few of us have had calls from the police advising us not to leave Bristol for the next few days. I guess the bastards used racial profiling and contact tracing to get us.'

Bianna, dropped her knife and looked at me with fear in her eyes. 'Could be nothing serious, routine police check,' I said to reassure them. 'But if the situation needs legal advice, we'll help you there, Ashbo.' The tension somewhat eased, we chatted about the protest and how it had gone. I wondered aloud if the protesters had further plans.

'Hell yes, I just remembered,' Ashbo perked up. 'Will you both come with me into the city centre tomorrow morning? I don't promise, but there may be a surprise awaiting us.'

How could we turn down such an intriguing invitation, especially when I was included?

~

So it was that we stood at Colston's vacated pedestal for the second time in a few days, in the midst of a confounded but largely amused crowd. I couldn't believe my eyes, for there on the pedestal someone had installed a statue of a magnificent black woman in a defiant pose – fist high in the air. 'Just look at that.' I beamed, hugging Bianna.

All she could do was utter 'Oh my god, Ashbo. Oh, my god, how superb.'

Ashbo laughed with pride. If he personally had a hand in installing this visual statement, he did not let on. 'That's the statue of my friend Jen Reid, one of the protest leaders,' he confided. 'Cast overnight in resin by one smart artist.'

The media was out in full force, and the police were consulting on their phones, clearly flummoxed for the moment. I doubted if the statue would find favour with the city fathers. It did, however, make me wonder if memorials ought to be installed to stand for all time when life and all else in the universe were so transient. Should traditionalists be allowed to cling to a white-washed history of colonisation and revere a dark and callous man like Edward Colston?

'Angel above, that's unbelievable.'

'What you on about now, mum?'

'It looks like Angela Davis. Almost a spitting image of her, I tell you.'

'Huh?

'No, you'd not know her, son. Much before your time.'

But *I* remembered the Black Power movement. Those heady days in the 1960s and 70s. It all came rushing back, names of firebrands like Bobby Serle, Eldridge Cleaver, Stokely Carmichael and Angela Davis.

'On yeah?'

'Yeah, you check her out, Ashbo. People say history repeats itself. So do pandemics. Old folks like us are certainly familiar with *unprecedented times.*'

I was tempted to add my bit to impress him. Something lofty and wise. *Ha yes, the tide of history is punctuated with high moments of black and brown struggle against white domination. There's been many a Geronimo, Jandamarra, Gandhi, Spartacus, Mandela, and Martin Luther King who'd risen and fallen for human rights.* Brilliant sentiment, I thought, but maybe just a little over the top for now. But worth remembering for a later chat with Ashbo. I felt pleased, but my smile went unnoticed beneath a scruffy homemade mask.

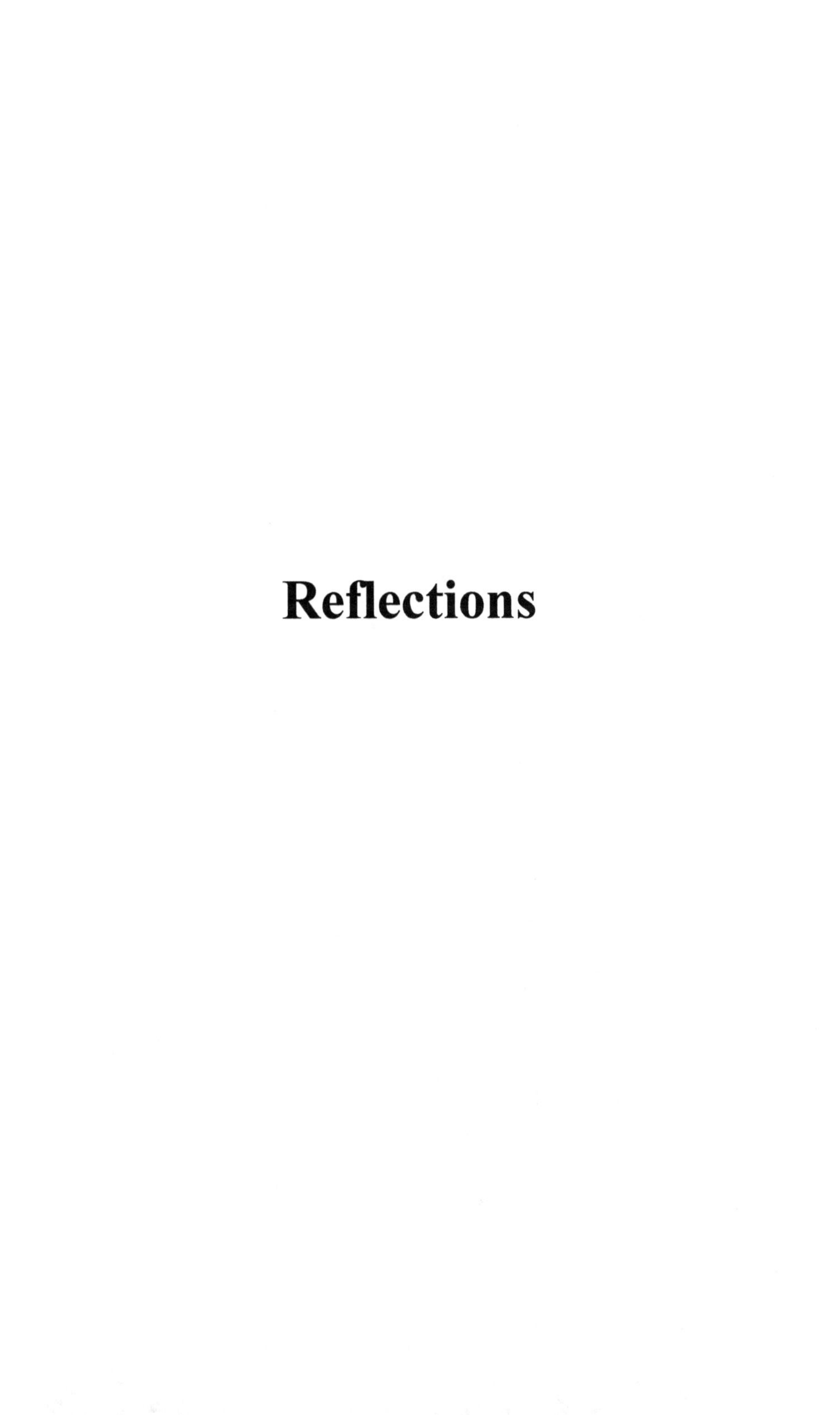

Reflections

Music That Stirs Me

If music be the food of love, play on. Shakespeare I sorely regret not having the talent for music and song. Nor had any others in my family. Yet I've always had a strange passion for the violin, the origins of which are murky and intriguing. But I suspect my father had something to do with it as I recall him telling me (why and when eludes me now) that the violin is a sacred instrument which needed to be treated with reverence. Before playing it, the violinist is expected to bathe and offer a solemn prayer at the polished brass *god-lamp*, once found in every traditional Tamil household. He's to beseech Saraswati, the goddess of music, to bless him and his violin. I may have been told this story at an impressionable age for the memory to have survived this long. I don't, however, recall my father actually owning a violin nor ever seeing him playing one - or any other instrument for that matter. So, it intrigues me to see him in a black and white group photo of young Indian musicians (probably taken in the 1930s) – all men posing with traditional instruments such as the tabla, violin, and a harmonium.

In my high school years, I got it into my head that I must learn to play the violin. The idea would have startled and unsettled my parents since my wilful intention had serious financial implications. Even a second-hand violin could be unaffordable. And what about the cost of weekly lessons? Had I given thought to that? My poor parents, however, indulged me even though it strained the household budget. I soon picked up a used instrument from a violin repair shop in Ajmeri Arcade owned by an Indian man called Sivaraja. He turned out to be a skilled violinist and a scholar of classical Indian music. And luckily, he took a kindly interest in my ambition and offered my father a good deal – even allowing him to pay in instalments. Sivaraja went further and found me a tutor, an elderly Polish man, Bogdan, who had a cramped studio in one of the laneways off Smith Street. By then I was working casually over weekends at Timol's Grocers and was able to contribute to the tuition fees.

My starry-eyed venture ended rather abruptly after just five sessions. Bogdan found me impossible to teach and promptly lost patience. He concluded that I didn't have an ear for music and that my fingers were quite inflexible. 'Leeesen,' he'd scream, his face contorted and flushed, and his Einstein-like hair collapsing in despair. I was mortified. No one had forewarned me that mastery of the violin necessitated tedious hours of practice in between sessions. I shied away from this essential requirement. Each time I picked up my violin at home, the awful screeching sounds frightened even the cats and ghosts in the neighbourhood. It upset our dog, Rover, who began howling. In reality, there was no place in the house where I could shut myself and let rip. My siblings complained that my infernal practice sessions distracted them from their homework. They felt embarrassed to assure neighbours that I wasn't trying to drown our cat in the toilet.

My father received a small refund for the violin. We soon forgot about the whole ridiculous episode. And I never again felt the urge to play another musical instrument. However, my fascination for violin music itself did not end there. It travelled with me to Australia when we migrated from South Africa in 1988. Now, Melbourne is noted for its buskers. There'd usually be a busking violinist somewhere in the city streets, especially over weekends and summer public holidays. As a pedestrian, I'd hear the sweet strings from a distance. My ears would immediately prick up and tug me along in the general direction.

Solo violin numbers are what delight me the most, but I don't mind solo playing on the cello or ukulele. I'm not that taken up by western classical music, except for perhaps segments of Beethoven's numbers. On the other hand, I'm a sucker for violin instrumentals of such pop classics as the Beatles or Simon & Garfunkel.

In certain circumstances, a person may respond to the violin as if it were possessed, capable of expressing all shades of human emotion reflecting the human condition. Here I'm reminded of the character Swann in Marcel Proust's first volume of his monumental novel *Remembrance of Things Past*. Swann attends a grand aristocratic ball and sees again the girl he's hopelessly in love with. But she rebuffs him at every turn with cold indifference. When a classical violin solo begins to be played, Swann finds himself drawn to the varying tempo and mood of the music and suffers much anguish believing that the violin was faithfully reflecting and amplifying all the shades of his heart ache. He hears in the music an enchanted voice: *Yes, yes, I understand Monsieur. I see how she makes you suffer*!

I was in my late 20s when I first read Proust. At the time, ironically, I myself was deeply entangled in an episode of unrequited love, and hence found myself readily sucked into Swann's emotional drama. Proust's fine description of the ebb and flow of the violin through strains of rapture and despair, spoke directly to me.

~

I'm also drawn to clustered voices in spiritual harmony, whether this be a gospel choir, Gregorian or Buddhist chanting, or an Indian bhajan. I find there's always something enthralling or uplifting when voices come together to render vocal music. I recall, for instance, a Qantas advert years ago on TV of a group of kids singing *Call Australia Home* from varied rugged landscapes, and the melody wafted upwards, echoing over the vastness of space.

There was a time back in South Africa, when I used to wait with anticipation for Pastor JF Rowlands and his Bethesda Temple choir taking up the Sunday Indian music hour on SABC radio, twice a year – at Easter and Christmas. I always found their accomplished singing (with violin and tabla accompaniment) joyful, passionate, and moving. The show usually included a couple of gospel songs in Tamil by a male singer. Although, we were staunch Hindus, my family had no qualms in appreciating Christian music. Years later, when I oversaw a residential village for children, Christmas spirit came early. Two good friends volunteered to rehearse the kids in singing Christmas carols. The one friend played the piano and the other lent us his baritone voice. Of course, how could I not join in – adding my discordant gusto to the lines I knew and mouthing the rest. The out-of-tune piano provided a unique flavour to the raucous madness. We had such memorable fun.

Since migrating to Australia in 1988, I developed a habit of turning on ABC TV on Sundays at 11.30 am, whenever possible, to watch a BBC production, *Songs of Praise*, a 30-minute live recording from some venue in Britain. Each show included a selection of psalms interspersed with a narrated history of the cathedral and the town in which it was located. But what fascinated me more was the earnest and varied faces of the congregation. The camera would pan clusters of singers - the elderly, men, women, the younger set and so on. If there was a person of colour among the congregation, the camera would return repeatedly to this face. Some singers would lift up their faces and sing with total spiritual absorption, while others, overly self-conscious whenever the TV camera came their way, would sing with affected gusto. I'd think their exaggerated facial expressions quite funny - eyes closed and mouths, lips and jaws working away in the earnest hope of making a most favourable impression of themselves on the watching world.

A while back, I had the rare opportunity to attend a Sunday morning mass at a massive Hill Song Church in Sydney. I was blown away by the colourful exuberance of the service with bursts of catchy, pop rendition of gospel music which got the congregation onto their feet, joining in song while rocking, swaying, and clapping in unison.

~

My wife is lucky to have grown up in a family steeped in a Hindu spiritual tradition. Hence, all her siblings learnt to sing popular bhajans (devotional songs) since childhood, from participating directly in multiple annual prayer events where bhajan singing (while sitting cross-legged) preceded formal rituals and offering. With their migration to Australia, the practice has continued in Melbourne, initially ensured by their mother, and now kept alive by their sister-in-law. So, for the past 32 years, I have been exposed to family bhajan sessions. deriving a great deal of joy in the process. I find many bhajans soulful and moving, although they are mostly in Sanskrit and their meaning somewhat obscure to me. There are bhajans always sung at funerals and at 'remembering the dead' ceremonies. I now not only look forward to these events but have become partial to a couple of the bhajans. I even have them copied on a tape. But here's the thing, I've still not learnt to sing bhajans. At best, I attempt to hum or mouth fragments. Am I just lazy to learn, tone deaf or simply dim-witted?

In preparing a file of expectations for my low-key funeral, I've made it known that including a couple of my favourite bhajans will certainly go well and send me off in good spirit. I may even consider this my final practice session - which should please my sister-in-law, the unanointed but undisputed taskmaster of family bhajan sessions. Should the family find a violin playing busker for the auspicious occasion, it will certainly be a rare treat – the icing on my coffin.

True Grit

Peter is our last surviving neighbour. In November 1989, twelve Anglo Australians from four households warmly embraced us dark-skinned South Africans as their new neighbours. In the intervening years, six have died and five have relocated, leaving Peter to be the last remaining face of old-world neighbourliness. With him turning 93, we are likely soon to draw the curtains on a memorable era.

One morning not so long ago, while busy on my computer, I heard a tentative knock at my front door. I hit the save button and hastened to check, only to see Peter hobbling away. He had delivered me a perfect cheesecake in a plastic see-through container - two dainty pieces sliced with great care. With each bite, I savoured its rich creamy texture and marvelled at the even thickness of the tawny biscuit base. This is certainly Peter the perfectionist. I've benefited from other exquisite culinary creations of his in the past, including Anzac biscuits, ginger tea cake and blood-plum jam. Being a perfectionist, he feels ashamed to share biscuits if they aren't *hard enough*, jam that's *a little runny* or his ginger cake if the ginger isn't obvious to the taste. On occasions, I've pleaded with him not to dump his *failures* but rather to allow me to feast on them. He mostly agreed, but with visible reluctance.

It amazes me how he keeps going, especially with a pretty crook body – gnarled and arthritic fingers, an eroded spine and a troublesome hip, following hip-replacement surgery. Perhaps it's his stoic disposition that helps him endure physical pain and endless lonely days of weariness, old age and sorrow. The sudden death of his wife, Gwen, a couple of years ago in a nursing home is an unimaginable loss. They had been married for almost 60 years and were much devoted to each other. She died from injuries sustained in a fall. Peter was traumatised by the event. He says he stood by helplessly while Gwen screamed in excruciating pain. Being a Sunday, the nursing home was operating with just two casual staff. No immediate medical help was available.

Come summer heat or winter chill, Peter would be outdoors weeding, *bent over* in his garden as he was no longer able to squat or kneel. Of late he seems almost obsessed to pick at any semblance of weeds in his otherwise *manicured* front and back gardens. Here am I thinking that an Australian *native garden* had to look a little unkempt and wild. But as a migrant, what do I know! After all, Peter is the one knowledgeable about native plants. He's the one who introduced me to *Kuranga*, a premier native plant nursery in the Dandenong Ranges.

Once, I was appalled to see him pushing a wheelbarrow with garden tools and a couple of pot plants – and his vital walking stick. *Oh my god*, I think, *he's now pushing his luck*. It was scary simply watching him doggedly at it, one unsteady step after another.

Whatever task he sets his mind on for that day, be it jam-making, composting, or cleaning his kitchen, he applies himself until the work's done, by which time, he'd have exhausted himself almost to death. '*Peter,*' I'd say with concern '*just look at you*!' His face would be deathly pale, eyes sunken and a voice almost inaudible. He would just about manage a feeble smile admitting that he was quite worn out and in some pain.

Peter recounts with pride how he came to build his house in Oakleigh in the fifties, with help from Marcus his brother-in-law, years younger than him. Together they had also built the house next door. But all that was in the past. Sadly, encroaching age has largely whittled away Peter's once remarkable hands-on capacity as a builder-cum-carpenter-cum-gardener. He now counts on his son-in-law, Jock, to help out with the heavy domestic stuff like pruning, mowing or un-jamming a sash window. As for Marcus, he died recently after two years in a nursing home. Being a very private person, Peter rarely speaks of Gwen or Marcus. He's not one to display emotion or express his feelings too readily – except when he berates right-wing politicians like Trump. Then his jaw would visibly tense up.

Peter confesses that he's partial to bread, cakes, and biscuits - all things sweet and nice. Yet he'd remind me when I invite him over for a chat '*no sugar in my tea, please.*' And a definite *no, no* to coffee. I recall once having to scrape the butter off his toast while apologising for assuming that the whole of mankind loved butter on toast! He simply loves salads and vegetables. Since we became his neighbours, he has also acquired an appetite for curries. So quite regularly I'd deliver him a curry pack of some sort. I'd enter unannounced through his permanently unlocked front door to find him seated in the kitchen. At once Peter's eyes would light up and he would offer me a cuppa, hoping for me to linger awhile for a chat.

The other day, with balmy spring in the air, he was pottering about outside his shed. Even from across the fence, I could tell that blood was oozing down his pale forehead. Alarmed, I rushed across to check if he was okay. He gave me a *no-big-deal* look as he put on his hearing aid. '*Oh that? Only a slight bump; just allowing the blood to cake-up.*' Peter's skin easily bruises since his treatment for cancer years earlier. And it's not uncommon for him, while out and about working, to knock an elbow or knee, hit his head on a jutting timber or cut a finger. Small matters for him. At times he isn't even aware that he has hurt himself. Peter has already had two falls in his garden in the last several months. I find this worrying, but Judy, his daughter who lives close by, is of the view that her father is very stubborn and detests being mollycoddled. '*Leave him be,*' she says. '*Should he keel over in his garden one day and die, so be it. For Peter, it would be a good death if he's found in his overalls.*' Getting out into the open and pottering about is what keeps him engaged and alive. He often tells me that he hates being shut in the house on his own and doing nothing. Perhaps he senses the whole house is still saturated with Gwen's presence – her voice, her smell, seated in her favourite chair or chatting on the phone with her best friend Dot.

I'm reminded of the poignant and understated lines from David Attenborough's 2010 memoir *Life in Air*. 'The thing is when you go around the house, you know that no matter how many doors you open, there's not going to be anybody there, and that's a pity.'

~

Peter is a *ten-pound Pom* from England, a beneficiary of the post-war migrant recruitment drive by the Commonwealth government to advance its *white Australia* policy. He arrived here from Hornchurch, a town south-east of London, at the age of 22, with a good friend. Both had completed their apprenticeship in shipbuilding. With the help of the local Shipwrights Union, they readily found work in the dockyard in Melbourne (now Docklands), where he remained until 1990 when a severe work injury compelled him into early retirement. Peter recalls having a hand in restoring the ship *Polly Woodside*, now a museum piece.

Peters' political inclinations are decidedly left wing. Even to this day he prefers reading *The Melbourne Age*, and identifies with the aspirations of indigenous peoples, refugees, and other under-dogs. He rails against the frontier wars where the white settlers did their darned best to eliminate the *First Australians*. Gwen told us once that she, as a young woman, was active in the Labour Party and participated in protests and rallies in the city. Peter would often join her. He also remembers helping at polling stations during State and Federal elections.

While frugal in many ways, Peter is still discerning about quality. His diet is modest. No more than a small bowl of corn flakes and a slice of toast for breakfast. He either skips lunch altogether because he 'can't be bothered,' or makes do with a sandwich with a generous slice of cheddar cheese or Roses orange marmalade. Dinner is his main meal. By midmorning, he has mostly decided on what it will be. Usually, an interesting combination of meat and vegetables, with our curry pack as a welcome alternative.

Without fail, Peter's up early on a Thursday morning to drive to Coles for his copy of the *Age* with the bonus *Green Guide* supplement which enables him to track the TV programs for the week. For his age, his eyesight is remarkably good, much better than mine. Before Covid, he was only too willing and appreciative to accompany us to the theatre or the cinema, only to doze off midway. The thing is, Peter hates snoozing during the day and prides himself for not succumbing to this common weakness in the elderly.

Peter never took to smoking and drinking like most of his shipwright mates even though he too suffered the harsh and demanding nature of his labour, more so in wet and freezing winter weather. No, he's not a church-going man. Never has been, he says, although he married Gwen in the church at the corner of Warrigal and Dandenong Roads.

I feel somewhat awed by Peter's varied interests and knowledge. How did he come to acquire them? Take for instance, his love of classical music. No, he says, no one in his family had had an ear for fine music. But he was drawn to classical music on the radio from an early age and remembers vividly travelling to London to a see a classical music performance at the Royal Albert Hall. Remarkable! Then there's his keenness and talent for bridge. For years, he met weekly with a group of elderly bridge players. But his hip and back problem set him back for a while. Later he learned that his team had recruited others to replace him and one other player who had died at the age of 96. Once Peter became quite enthusiastic to teach me this superior card game. But I quit after two lessons as I found the rules too complex and a little beyond my grasp. I could tell that Peter was quite disappointed because, I guess, he'd hoped to pick up his bridge passion again with me as a partner.

Covid has turned our familiar world on its head and driven us into living unnatural virtual lives. How fortunate, then, to still have Peter as a dependable, friendly neighbour. I have always enjoyed the occasional impromptu chitchats over the fence, and our mutual sharing and informal hospitality. The awareness is ever present, however, that all this will soon end. In Tennyson's words: *The old order changeth yielding place to new.* I find it remarkable that Peter has no qualms about dying. He is very much for euthanasia, that people ought to have control over their lives. And he has no stomach for religious scruples. 'Hell? What hell? he asks vehemently. 'Just a load of rubbish if you ask me.'

The face of Melbourne's rapidly changing. This is evident in Hughesdale as well. We were the first couple of *colour* to settle in Darling Street. Now, we have a Chinese neighbour – a middle-aged couple with a son aged 30 years. Chung speaks good English, but not his parents. Chung and I have become nodding acquaintances in the last several months. As he is young, Chung may be around for a lot longer than Peter – or me, for that matter. But one never can tell. Nothing is for sure in these uncertain times! When he joined me on a walk around the neighbourhood the other day, Chung told me with a casual laugh that he was thinking of joining the Australian Navy. There you go, I thought, he too will probably disappear soon.

Gandhi: Epiphanies and Makeovers

Would Gandhi have read Hamlet? He probably had as he seems to have picked up on Polonius's advice to his young son, Laertes, who's about to set off to study in Paris. Always dress well son, says Polonius, because 'the apparel oft proclaims the man.'

Young Gandhi, when about twenty years old, was sent by his influential family to London to train as a barrister. On his return to his hometown in Gujarat, India, Gandhi struggled to make a living as a lawyer. As a result, his family shipped him off to South Africa to help one of their Indian business friends in legal matters.

At the end of three weeks of a rough sea passage, Gandhi arrived in Port Natal (Durban). He retrieved his favourite outfit carefully packed in his travelling case - an outfit he had purchased in London after graduation. In donning it, the young lawyer clearly wished to impress his new employer and other traders likely to turn up to meet him. Gandhi also, by his preferred dressing, wanted to make a statement that he wasn't just any ordinary Indian lawyer, but an *English*-trained barrister. The very crème de la crème.

So it is that in a photo taken of him soon after his arrival in Durban at age twenty-four, Gandhi poses arms firmly folded, supremely confident. Here, despite his brown skin, he proclaims himself to be a dapper Victorian gentleman. Tall and lean-faced, piercing eyes, self-assured. He's dressed in a 3-piece Savile-row suit, raised collar and striped tie. I notice a lapel badge. His soot black hair, with an off-centre part, is carefully plastered. Above all, the stand-out feature in this photo is his flourishing moustache - shaped like the horns of a bull, curved and inverted.

Fatima Meer says in her 1970 biographical novel about Gandhi (*Apprenticeship of a Mahatma*) that his host was quite put off by the young man's dandy-like elegance, and 'secretly wondered what he would do with him.' Would he turn out to be a 'white elephant?'

~

Within months things took a dramatic turn. Gandhi had a rude awakening one evening when he was thrown off a train by the police near Pietermaritzburg. A White man objected to a *coolie* enjoying the comforts of a 'whites-only' first class coach. Did he not know his place?

Gandhi was headed for Pretoria on a legal mission for his employer. He had believed all along that he was a proud citizen of the British Empire, a loyal subject of Queen Victoria. But now stranded and shivering in the night air of a deserted railway station, Gandhi woke to the fact that he wasn't exactly a White man. So incensed was he, that he resolved there and then to campaign against all colonial era racial laws and practices in Natal that restricted fellow countrymen.

I couldn't say if Gandhi immediately thereafter dumped all his English-style clothes into the bin.

A few years later, in June 1904, Gandhi had his second epiphany – again on a train. On this occasion he was on his way back to Durban from the Transvaal. A White friend, Henry Pollak, apparently gave him a copy of John Ruskin's *Unto This Last*, a collection of essays on a socialist world view. Later, Gandhi wrote that this event proved to be a turning point in his life. 'It gripped me, and I couldn't get any sleep that night. I was determined to change my life.' He, thereafter, came to believe that the way he chose to live his life would have implications for the future of humanity; and that all work was of equal value. As an English trained barrister, he was no different to the indentured labourer. He would, henceforth, live his new vision in action. Gandhi soon emulated Ruskin by establishing the Phoenix Settlement, a work commune outside Durban where he experimented with a new way of frugal spiritual living.

~

Gandhi became increasingly aware that the indentured Indian labour system was in fact 'perilously close to slavery.' Zainab

Priya Dala (*What Gandhi Didn't See*, 2018), however, claims that Gandhi hadn't personally visited the sugar plantations outside Durban to witness first-hand how Indians were being exploited. In any event, in 1914, Gandhi made a conscious and visible effort to identify with the indentured Indians and their suffering. He resorted to a makeover so austere and drastic that he no longer resembled his former self - at least in physical appearance. He said that only by dressing like the indentured man would he be able to identify with them fully and be accepted and trusted by them.

In the above photo, Gandhi stands erect with a bamboo staff in his right hand, his hair cropped almost to his scalp, and face clean-shaven. The absence of his moustache is telling. He wears a typical Indian working man's clothes. A long-sleeved white cotton tunic (kurta) descending below the knee, under which he wears a lungi or dhoti. A hessian carrying pouch, with a long shoulder strap, rests loosely on his hip. Gandhi stares wide-eyed into the camera, almost like a stunned mullet. What he had done to himself, he wonders, in sacrificing his carefully cultivated image of a barrister?

~

Upon returning to India for good in 1914, Gandhi, however, wasted little time in reverting to the traditional costume of his birthplace, Kathiawar – dhoti, long coat, a stole on his shoulders and a white turban. His handlebar moustache is back and flourishing.

Gandhi had his third epiphany in September 1921 while travelling by train from Madras to Madurai. If I wish to champion the cause of the poor and dispossessed masses of my country, he thought, I need to show it in my dress. Their poverty must be my poverty. So it was that he came to the momentous decision to shed almost all his fashionable clothes, making do with no more than a white home-spun cotton loin cloth.

Henceforth, Gandhi lived, day and night, in his dhoti and

shawl. In the photo above he is naked waist up, bare knees down, head shaven, and in sandals. A pair of utility glasses, round-lensed wire-rimmed, completes the iconic lean image of Gandhi in his later years.

Gandhi, intentionally or otherwise, projects an image of a sramana of ancient Vedic India, an ascetic or renunciate who fends for himself, surviving on bare essentials.

Here we have a Gandhi who appears to have completed his journey of mental and spiritual transformation, which is vindicated in his stark outward appearance. By his bold stride he asserts his newfound soul force, which he will harness soon enough to mount a relentless campaign aimed at ridding India of the British Imperial yoke. He clutches a copy of the daily newspaper, hefty with politics of the day. By his expression, I would guess he was anticipating a good morning's read.

Gandhi stuck to this garb even when he travelled to Britain and had tea with King George V. Churchill was, however, scandalised. He referred to him disparagingly as 'that half-naked fakir.' A great irony is that today his scantily clad statue stands in Parliament Square in London in proximity to his archrivals Churchill and Smuts, probably causing them much discomfort.

~

In his search for ultimate truth, Gandhi was driven by a single-minded zeal: If he desired the world to change for the better in a truly profound way., why not start the change-process in himself? Become the role model. In this pursuit, Gandhi underwent phases of political and spiritual transformation, attempting to make visible his inner metamorphoses by dramatically changing his dress and appearance. Oddly enough, however, he seems to have retained his characteristic moustache – the last vestige of his original self.

Port Arthur: A Beauty Born of Pain

Ocean cruises are not everyone's cup of tea. Even so I couldn't resist the special pre-Christmas offer of a short cruise on the Golden Princess. So, a fortnight before the annual commercialised insanity of Yuletide, my wife and I escaped for some peace and quiet on a six-day cruise. The round trip from Melbourne to Tasmania would include day stops in Hobart and Port Arthur.

Our first shore excursion was Port Arthur. Inclement weather was predicted. I felt a little reluctant to leave the comforts of the ship. Sight-seeing in wet weather wouldn't be much fun. Nevertheless, we dared ourselves to risk it since the weatherman was known to err. We joined the disembarking queue, and as we stepped onto the gangplank, the rain found us. An overcast and sombre morning accompanied by intermittent drizzle. Out came my umbrella and my wife pulled on her hoodie.

Four lifeboat-sized vessels (called tenders) operated a shuttle, ferrying hundreds of passengers from the ocean liner to the jetty, a 40-minute journey over choppy waters. The make-shift tarp over the entrance flapped and strained. The tender lunged and rose in manic regularity as it cut through the surf. Most unpleasant for those of us who sat nearby as we caught the jets of spray.

~

I pulled out and glanced again at the on-board brochure on Port Arthur, reading the lurid bits to my wife. 'savage cliffs, brooding mountains'; 'impenetrable prison'; 'prisoners forced to labour'; 'shark-infested waters'; 'spine-tingling tales'; 'poor souls who perished here'; 'over 1000 convicts buried in the eerie cemetery'; and 'haunted grounds.' After this kind of disturbing litany, why would anyone wish to disembark? Well, here's the thing, the brochure's enticing claim was that Port Arthur boasted 'the reputation of being one of the most popular vacation and sightseeing destinations.' That's marketing for you. Horror sells.

~

I stepped ashore with mixed feelings. The massacre of April 1996 was uppermost on my mind. Yet the brochures provided by the cruise ship, Golden Princess, dealt almost entirely with the convict settlement, now a UNESCO heritage site. The remains of the penal settlement, although some distance away, were still visible. The complex of skeletal ruins and restored buildings stood along the near horizon, with tree-lined grassy lawns spread out in front like an apron.

We hastened from the jetty seeking shelter from the rain. A signboard listed the things to be visited. We chose a path leading to the Visitor Centre, treading gingerly over squelching mud and shallow puddles. The manicured grounds fell away on our left, then rose gently again to the edge of the historic ruins, where we saw visitors standing singly, in pairs, and clumps. Hooded or with umbrellas.

Others appeared to be drifting about or proceeding to the next vantage point.

~

I speculated that not all who had come onshore would be captivated by Port Arthur and its colourful penal settlement history. Some, with sound knowledge of its past, would use the visit to glean as much as they could. The actively curious would hear the account from guides, and perhaps be moved. And what of the indifferent ones? I guess they'd enjoy the pleasures of wandering about aimlessly, simply stretching their legs or looking for ideal spots for selfies.

~

When bored, they'd drift to the café, use the washrooms, and generally while away time. Later I'd find the large café area at the Visitor Centre humming with enthusiastic patrons doing justice to the varied spread on the menu. How could they manage such feasting after all that indulgence aboard ship?

~

Just as the path began veering right, a large building of modern design became partially visible.

'Ah, that must be the Visitor Centre,' I said.

'But see, not everyone is making for the Centre,' said my wife.

A group of four or five people hesitated at a plaque, turned, and headed right, away from the Visitor Centre. On coming up behind them, we noticed a narrow path disappearing into dense shrubs, drenched and glistening. We followed without a second thought as the plaque pointed us to the Port Arthur Memorial Site.

In twenty metres or so, we came upon it. Here on a fateful day, which unfolded much like any other day, 35 visitors, casually relaxing in a café or nearby, had their lives snuffed out in a nightmarish instant. Pursued and shot with vengeful intent by a very disturbed man, who also shot and wounded 23 others. A catastrophe of mind-boggling proportion. "How could such a thing happen here?' were the words that reverberated across a traumatized and deeply troubled nation.

~

I'm sure others feel much the same as I do when confronted by TV news images (or hear stories) of horrendous deaths and maiming, occurring suddenly and when least expected – especially of children and families. It numbs me every time, and makes me want to look away, run for cover. Such were my reactions when I read Leigh Sales' book *Any Ordinary Day*. Here, she picked up on personal stories of unutterable pain, suffering and loss experienced by people. She invited a sample of such people to explain to her, individually, how each had in his/her own remarkable way, journeyed from paralytic darkness and despair into some semblance of light. How was it that a rare few found such courage to endure? To raise their faces yet again to the sun. I guess Leigh Sales was in search of the alchemy of ultimate human survival.

According to psychologist Jordan Petersen from Toronto University, instead of becoming all 'bitter and corrupted', these people 'orient themselves to be propelled forward', forging for themselves, once more, tolerable personal lives.

~

Walter Mikac was one among those Leigh Sales interviewed. When reading his testimony, I put the book down a couple of times and took a breather in my garden. Mikac tells of how his wife, Nanette and daughters Alannah, six, and Madeline, three, were shot and killed at Port Arthur, in the blink of an eyelid - even as Nanette pleaded for her girls to be spared. Mikac says he heard the shots from the nearby golf course where he was absorbed in a game but, at that moment, didn't give it a second thought.

Such an austere and confined setting, I thought. The memorial site was miniscule in comparison to the lavish and manicured vastness of the convict heritage site we had just passed. Cloistered was the word that came to mind. It conjured up for me a place cold and wet and forlorn like a cemetery in an ancient country churchyard. I felt a silent shiver. The abandoned and roofless Broad Arrow Café, a modest memorial garden, reflection pool, and a simple cross with the names of those killed. The cross itself seemed no more than a rough piece of wood stripped from a tree with little done to shape it into perfection.

Was this all? Did it do justice to the enormity of the tragedy? Did it not need a defining image like Munch's the *Scream* or of Picasso's *Guernica*?

It surprised me that the café was now just a shell, resembling the burnt ruins of the prison and penitentiary complex. I later learnt that, in the process of it being demolished, someone had suggested that the Cafe be retained (in its partially dismantled form) as part of the memorial site. When I stepped into it for a moment, I thought I sensed faint cries drifting in and out of the windowless openings.

~

By the time we arrived at the Visitor Centre, the intermittent rain had largely vanished, replaced by patches of fluffy clouds and pale-blue sky. The building itself was at two levels, with a museum and café claiming much of the space. Information to tourists was dispensed through a hatch. A spacious entrance hall but no information counter. It didn't make sense.

As there was nothing much of interest to us here, we set off from the Centre to explore the major heritage site. Not all the paths leading to the ruins, cottages and gardens were sealed. Hence, we skirted the muddy paths by chancing it and walking on the lawn.

Whichever path we took, wherever we stood, the view we had was panoramic. I could imagine the comfort and pleasure derived by the fortunate prison warders.

~

Government personnel and entrepreneurs once lived here with their families ensuring its prosperity. The reality was that this colonial resort was the product of convict labour. By dint of their sheer toil and sweat, convicts had transformed an area of virgin forest into a thriving settlement for a privileged few. I'm almost certain no prisoner, transported and dumped here against his will (and on questionable offences), would have considered it a blessing to breathe the air of Port Arthur.

I simply couldn't reconcile the fact that such a beguiling landscape of manicured gardens, elegant trees and shrubs, undulating lawns, and meandering paths had also been a place of unimaginable brutality, hardship, of countless wasted lives. But why am I conflicted? Hadn't I read or heard of the battlefields of Flanders, yet another place of compelling beauty, where hundreds of young men were slaughtered, or died from disease, starvation or rotting wounds? I'm told, even to this day, the poppies bloom there in blood-red profusion. On a still morning or as dusk settled, you may still sense anguish in the air. A longing for home.

There was something inherently deceptive (even fraudulent) about all this lofty grandeur. Were the masters and benefactors of the penal settlement simply living a lie? Intentionally? Are we who now flock to Port Arthur to receive an intimate account of its disturbing history doing so much like going to see a horror movie for the fearful thrill it would give us?

~

Those who lorded over the lives of unfortunate prisoners had contrived a brutal system of labour exploitation, forged a thriving industrial enterprise based on mining, logging and shipbuilding. Manpower was free and plentiful. Any number of prisoners could be asked for from Britain and the colonies. Floggings and solitary confinement were the popular method of coercion – to break the spirit of convicts who did not readily comply. The Isle of the Dead was the convict cemetery with over a thousand unmarked and unsung graves.

Over time, unfortunate survivors grew feeble or became insane. Hence a lunatic asylum – yet another happy addition to the complex.

Beneath the idyllic gloss of Port Arthur also lies buried the story of the indigenous people who, I'm told, have virtually disappeared from the population – having been hunted, sexually exploited and exterminated, or having died of white man's diseases.

~

We wandered about and had a closer look at a few of the buildings. What struck me was how well they had been designed and constructed – the lintels of sturdy timber, the stones cut and laid so precisely, the windows uniformly spaced. All accomplished by the most skilful convict labour. I found the sandstone walls particularly soft and aesthetic. It reminded me of the ancient ruins of Palmyra in Syria, desecrated by ISIS not so long ago. We also marvelled at the huge cathedral built with similar diligence, now just a fire-gutted shell.

Devastating fires in 1895 and 1897 had ravaged Port Arthur and within hours reduced to ruins what the convicts had taken years of blood and toil to construct. Remarkably, though, the fires appeared to have only served to enhance the aesthetic appeal of the complex. In the words of Irish poet WB Yeats, catastrophic events sometimes produce profound outcomes.

...changed, changed utterly:
A terrible beauty is born.

~

All through history, fire has served communities as a ritual of cleansing and regeneration. In this sense, I wonder if the fires at Port Arthur provided for healing and closure. If this was not the case, where then had all that ocean of pain, and suffering gone? There's only the beauty of the landscape now, and the stories of horror to thrill the voyeuristic appetite of tourists.

~

I came to realise that there were three distinct stories of inflicted pain and deprivation at Port Arthur – that suffered by the convicts, that of the victims of the 1996 massacre, and that endured by the first nations. Port Arthur tourism appeared to promote the convict narrative, while glossing over the other two. In reality, however, these are not three competing stories of pain. They are, in fact, bound by a compelling theme from which our gaze may not be averted. It's a universally enduring theme: "man's inhumanity to man," as expressed by Robert Burns the Scottish poet.

~

Our tender eased itself away from the jetty, taking us back to the luxurious Golden Princess, a make-believe world far removed from the reality of our everyday existence. The imposing sun-drenched ruins of Port Arthur receded with the disappearing shoreline. A final thought came to mind before I stepped aboard and surrendered to indulgence and torpor.

The unsavoury truth seemed all too obvious. We are, inherently, primitive animals. The line that separates the compassionate human from the brutish beast cuts through the human heart.

South African Memories

Baxter

As a teenager, I treated dogs with disdainful indifference. Rover was an off-white and brown mongrel my family kept as a watchdog in Mayville, South Africa in the 1950s. We had him chained during the day in a sheltered recess under the stairs, next to a kennel built by father. We treated Rover like an animal, kept him at a distance, never indulging him with kind words or gestures, strictly adhering to a *master-dog* relationship. We fed him mostly household scraps. As a faithful guard dog, he curled up at the back steps at night.

Rover used to roam at night and was involved in many fights pursuing a bitch in heat. At some point, he dislocated the upper joint of a hind leg. Vets were unknown at the time. Oh well, he should not have got himself into fights, may have been our attitude. Hence, he was pretty much expected to heal himself. The dislocation caused the hind leg to fold and shorten permanently, leaving us with a crippled three-legged guard dog. Rover moved in a warped manner, like an unaligned car pulling to the one side.

On occasions, I would forget to chain Rover before leaving for school, and he would follow me to the bus stop where I'd meet with school mates. 'Stupid dog,' I'd say in embarrassment as I'd hurl stones at Rover and threaten: 'Go home! Bugger off. Now!' He would stop, gaze at me woefully, turn reluctantly and hobble back. I'd then dismiss him from my thoughts.

One late morning when I had failed to chain Rover, the municipal stray-dogs van apparently came upon him. This was the story of a neighbour. We never saw Rover again. Now, upon reflection, I feel it was an act of mercy for him to have been put down. Rover had truly lived a *dog's life*.

~

My feelings for dogs changed dramatically soon after I married. More precisely, it was when my wife and I adopted Baxter, a black spaniel. He became a rare companion who made me proud. This explains why I felt as if I was *self-harming* when I had him put down. It happened in Durban 32 years ago, days before we migrated to Australia. Even now I get a little emotional whenever I speak of this painful event, justifying why he had to be put down. He was too old to be taken with us, I would explain. He would not cope with being quarantined in Australia. And leaving him behind, would be abandonment the second time around. As I continued speaking, the feeling of distress would well up deep in me and threaten to surface as visible tears. I would then turn away from whoever I was conversing with, making as if I were cleaning my glasses or checking my phone.

Baxter was the only pet my wife and I ever owned together as a couple. He came to us quite unexpectedly. A few years into our marriage, we moved into a two-storey unit in Briardale, our first home. I do not think we planned then on acquiring a pet dog. The story is not entirely clear to me, but as far as I can tell, either my mother-in-law or one of my wife's sisters, had heard of two dogs in Isipingo urgently needing a home. The owners, a couple related to my wife, had migrated a year earlier, leaving behind their dogs in the temporary custody of an elderly aunt, who was already saddled with a few dogs of her own. It seems we were persuaded to assist since my wife had long experience with pets. She grew up in a dog loving family and retained fond memories of many past canine pets.

And so it was that the two *orphaned* dogs came to us in Briardale. However, Mrs Singh, our next-door neighbour, was keen to care for sunny-faced Jumbo with a fluffy tawny coat. Fair enough, we thought, with us both working full-time, attending to one pet may realistically be enough for us.

Both the dogs were fully grown male spaniels, only a little taller than a poodle. It seems Jumbo came with his name, while we chose to call our dog Baxter. I really cannot recall if we didn't like the name he was given, or if we weren't told his name. Equally puzzling is how we came by the name *Baxter*. No clues whatsoever here. As he was black, the kids and some adults mistakenly began calling him Blackster, which amused us no end. But we didn't always correct them.

Initially, Baxter was one very insecure dog with a soulful face. He sulked and cowered from us, showed little interest in food placed before him and seemed unmotivated to explore his environment. There were other tell-tale signs of neglect and abandonment. His coat was coarse, smelly, and riddled with fleas. It took many months for Baxter to settle, adjust to his new home and surroundings, and learn to trust us.

Gradually over months, all this gave way and Baxter soon

became a contented pet, taking fully to us and our social habits. Baxter, my wife, and I formed a threesome. He spent most of my working hours with me at Lakehaven Children's Home where I worked. Baxter basked in the playful attention showered on him by the children. He was free to roam the expansive campus of buildings and open grounds, to explore the bushes beyond. At other times, I would catch him snoozing, curled up beneath my desk or lying embarrassingly on his back with all four legs in the air and his mouth open as wide as an air-vent.

Whenever I went about on my daily rounds inspecting the cottages at Lakehaven, the grounds, gardens and outdoor facilities, Baxter would either be at my heel or run ahead, inadvertently alerting staff of my approach. 'Bala's on his way,' would be the message relayed on the grapevine. A visitor, upon seeing Baxter close by, would often remark 'Lovely dog. Yours?'

'Yes,' I'd say with pride. 'That's Baxter.' And Baxter would prick up his ears at the very mention of his name and wag his tail with anticipation.

But things were not always hunky dory. I recall a couple of occasions at Lakehaven when he caused me acute annoyance and embarrassment. Both times it was just before a monthly meeting of the Lakehaven Board, just as I was rushing about finalising minutes, agenda, and reports, and checking on refreshment. And perhaps when I was a little uneasy that one or two nosey board members might turn up early to go on a *casual* walkabout without first announcing their presence.

There was a terrible stench at my feet. 'Oh my god,'

screamed my secretary. It was Baxter, his hairy bottom dripping with shit - diarrhoea! I gritted my teeth, lifted him in a fierce hold and rushed him to a rear garden tap. A horde of excited kids followed, some pinching their noses, others giggling or whispering in disgust. I desperately hoped that a roving board member would not catch me in the act.

~

At the end of a working day, I would simply call out 'Baxter, let's go' and he'd turn up like a bullet from somewhere, jump into the back seat of my VW, his tongue hanging out a mile, his eyes and ears alert with the thrill of travel. Off we would go. This was the cue for Baxter's barking frenzy. At times, I would have a back window partially opened so that he would stick out his snout and direct his bark at pedestrians and other dogs – rather than yapping into my ear and suffocating me with his breath, as rancid as the steam off a compost bin.

There was this occasion when I stopped briefly at a friend's place in Bakerville Gardens. I got home, parked and went indoors, greeting my wife as usual. 'Where's Baxter?' she asked quite casually. I froze. 'Oh bugger, I must have left him behind.' It was a mad dash to where I had stopped on my way home. And there was Baxter at my friend's house, frantically running back and forth on the street.

The one other time he was accidently left behind was when we were invited to dinner by our close friends, a married couple. They lived on the same street as us, no more than five houses away. After dinner and several drinks, we walked back home a little inebriated and just about ready to hit the bed. As we opened the door to let ourselves in, the phone rang. I rushed to picked it up.

'Hey,' says the wife with a merry laugh. 'You forgot Baxter. Poor chap's frantic.'

'How silly of us! But what a stupid dog. Doesn't he know where we live?' I justified my irritation and said I certainly was not going over to fetch him.

'So sorry,' she responded in a mock seriousness. But I could just picture her amused face.

I said, 'Hold the phone close to him so he'll hear me whistle.' The next moment we saw him come bounding down the road, his slick black form just visible in the light of the moon. He crashed through the open door and right into me. The phone was still in my hand. I heard our friends in stitches, having a good laugh.

~

Baxter was finicky about food. More like he did not much like eating or to be *seen* eating. Not sure which. We had only realised that he hadn't quite done with the previous week's bone when, upon settling onto our settee to watch the TV news, I got this awful sweet stench of rotting meat. And there buried in the crevasse of two cushions I find the culprit – Baxter's buried bone. On being severely reprimanded, he would creep away with woebegone eyes and ears limp with contrition.

Whenever I found his bowl of food untouched, I'd pin Baxter between my knees as I knelt over him and force-feed him, a morsel at a time which he'd meekly swallow.

Bath time was always a drama. 'Bath time,' we would sing out invitingly. Even so, Baxter would shoot up and bolt. We would have to hunt him down from some hidden part of the house and virtually drag him to the bathtub. Once done, I would dry and wrap him in his towel and carry him gingerly to the outside lawn area, drop him and promptly make distance. If I was slow at it, I'd get the full blast of the spray, as he shakes himself vigorously.

It was a sweltering summer day. We were at dinner in the kitchen with all the windows and doors fully open. The usual sounds drifted in. Pedestrians chatting and laughing as they passed by, and, of course, speeding traffic. Suddenly the familiar and ordinary was shattered by the fearful screeching of a motorbike in strife, accompanied by the most blood curdling howl of a dog followed by a spate of hysterical yelps. 'Baxter!' we shouted simultaneously as we dashed out and up the driveway, expecting the worse. Kids and adults tumbled out of the adjoining flats and crowded around the dramatic scene. A motorcyclist, in an Ashwin's Discount Pharmacy jacket, was in the process of removing his helmet and face-shield. Baxter was on the ground twitching and wailing. A concerned voice in the crowd shouted, 'Rush him to the vet.'

'Not me! Not my fault.' The sweat-face motorcyclist breathed heavily. 'The stupid dog. Rushed me from behind. You see, you see.' The man pointed to a tear in his pants at the ankle.'

'But you kicked him, yah?' My full attention was on Baxter. He whimpered each time I touched him. He's done for, I thought. We rolled him onto a piece of carpet and settled him on the back seat of our VW. Baxter kept up his pathetic feeble whimpering as my wife sat with him speaking soothing words.

Once placed on the vet's examination table, Baxter fell stone silent. No amount of poking and plodding by the vet elicited a sound. When encouraged, he promptly stood up, spotted us, and wagged his tail. 'Just shock,' was the vet's verdict. 'What!' exclaimed my wife in disbelief. 'You wimp!' She could have hit Baxter.

In fairness to Baxter, there was at least one time when he acted with bravado. I was woken one night by frantic barking just outside the bedroom. Baxter was halfway up the stairs to the upper level and directing his barking at the dimly lit courtyard, beyond the double glass doors in our lounge. I could not quite make out what had triggered the barking, until I noticed a faint movement in the shadows. Next moment, a dark form dropped like a sack of potatoes from a parapet,

96

scaled over the adjacent security gate, and disappeared. All in a split second. Baxter certainly redeemed himself in our eyes, proving to be a faithful guard dog after all, not just a mutt, lovable but useless.

~

My moment with Baxter at the point of his dying was an infinitely profound and unsettling experience. I still retain a vivid sense of holding Baxter down by his tummy, feeling his plump warmth like that of a child. I felt his wriggle to break free. The primordial instinct to clutch onto life at all costs. I felt his body tremble with fear of imminent death. At that moment, he and I were one. His terror entered me.

But how very swiftly *vital life* ebbs away, crossing a shadow-line, turning a pulsating heart into a disposable lump. This was for me a foretaste of my dying, my near-death experience. An enduring memory etched in every cell of my being.

I drove away from the veterinary clinic overwhelmed by the thought that Baxter was no more. A final act of merciful abandonment.

Landscapes, Memory and Me

Any landscape is a condition of the spirit
Henri Frederic Amiel

The first few years of life in Australia were painful. My wife and I felt quite homesick. On our long Sunday drives to get a feel of Melbourne and beyond, I would catch myself saying things like: 'Oh, doesn't this remind you of the 'Valley of a Thousand Hills'? or 'This is so much like the market gardens along the Umgeni River in Springfield.' It took many years before I grew to love the wildness of the Australian bush. I, too, would be appalled when recurring summer wildfires laid waste vast swathes of natural forest of gum, wattle, mountain ash and eucalyptus. I, too, would feel the grief when my eyes fell upon miles and miles of stripped and blackened trees standing gaunt across the horizon. But I guess I would be considered un-Australian to nurse a single lantana bush in my garden when this shrub, so prolific in Durban, was classified as 'one of the worst invasive weeds in Australia.' When my lantana bush bursts into bright orange-yellow flowers in summer, I would invariably be transported back to the landscape of my childhood years which so shaped my identity.

'Okay class, paint anything you wish today,' announced the teacher to my delight. It was the weekly art class again at my primary school in Cato Manor. Seldom were we given a free hand. I loved painting outdoor sceneries, and my choice now was the Durban Bluff. When fishing at the Durban Docks, my father had pointed it out to me. It was as close and as large as a Union Castle passenger-ship I had seen at Maydon Wharf. The Bluff was a prominent jutting land mass, a ridge that embraced and sheltered the Durban Bay from the threatening storms of the Indian Ocean. It stretched out like a sunning crocodile. From Cato Manor, we would normally go into the city by an Indian owned bus, and then walk for about forty minutes to get to Maydon Wharf. And if we wished to get across the bay to the Bluff itself, we would have to do so by ferry. The image of the bay hemmed by the Bluff was considered striking and unique, and hence attracted the attention of notable artists.

~

The Durban Bluff

Gilbert Sir was our art teacher. He would wear a double-breasted suit, tightly buttoned. He was a tall, urbane man with thinning hair neatly plastered back, and a face that readily

100

creased into a broad smile. He praised my watercolour landscape of the Bluff and submitted it for the Annual Natal Indian Schools Art Exhibition sponsored by the Department of Education. I could not conceal my pride, more so when on a school excursion to the exhibition, I spotted my painting displayed prominently on a wall with other submissions. Mine had a blue sticker at the bottom right with the words 'Highly Commended' - fourth prize in the Junior category.

There were many other such images familiar to me in my childhood and youth that still linger in my memory – including some reminders of emotion-charged events. Take for instance, the fenced field next to where we lived in Cato Manor. Dimly through the winter mist, I would often see cows grazing on dew-drenched grass. Once my sister Kamala and I crawled under the barbed wire fence to collect fresh cow-dung, easily spotted by the smelly steam rising from the squishy blobs. We would hand the heavy bucket of pickings to my mother who'd be keeping a wary eye on the other side of the fence. Later we would see her smearing the stuff over a dusty patch of earth in the backyard to firm it up. I distinctly recall, too, a contraption of bamboo poles on this field, complete with rope and bucket. Many a time my sister and I would stand at the fence intrigued by how the farmer lowered the bucket into a well and drew water and emptied it into a network of shallow make-shift channels in his field of mealie crops and pumpkin. Father called the contraption a *shaduf* – which I learnt years later originated in ancient Egypt.

These recollections of landscapes were the very stuff in which I swam, like fish fully immersed in and sustained by the ocean. I consider *landscape* to be in the fullest cultural sense embracing places, traditions and ordinary activities of family and community. Landscape nurtured in me a sense of belonging and influenced how I thought of who I was. Consciousness is said to be embedded in context. As Philip Simmons (*Learning to Fall: The Blessings of an Imperfect Life,* 2000) says: '*the world moves through us as we move through the world.*' Yes, I did not exist in a vacuum but thrived in a dynamic and rich environment, a blend of constructed neighbourhoods and natural landscape. Cato Manor (on the fringes of the city of Durban) for me was a vibrant, flourishing community. I lived and journeyed through this landscape of colour, movement, sound, smell and so much more. Tropical Durban was mostly warm. Not many of us owned cars or even bicycles, hence people were always out and about walking everywhere. Old men would be seen toiling in their modest vegetable gardens, women hanging out washing on make-shift clothes lines - bright patterned saris and skirts, people exchanging news with curious neighbours over their common boundary fences, children engaged in excited street play (hop-scotch, marbles, or gully-tundha – an improvised village cricket), itinerant vendors peddling clothes or kitchenware from house to house and, of course, dogs of all shapes, colours and sizes indulging their barking skills all day and night. Any moving shape or shadow was worth a barking frenzy. On weekends there was bound to be traditional music emanating from someone's backyard – shrill singing accompanied by the tabla and harmonium. Ah, that could be a wedding or a religious event, I would speculate.

Much cooking occurred on woodfires, the enticing aroma

of curries, especially chicken curry, drifting on the evening breeze. Since the community was closely knit, we were often invited to participate in the festivities. At dawn on Sundays, when most people were still asleep, I would hear the plaintive cry of a peacock rising heavenwards. I would have an immediate picture of the white-washed Cato Manor temple on a hilltop across Second River where several peacocks roamed in a shaded mango grove.

Somehow it did not seem to matter much then that Cato Manor was impoverished, constrained by years of white-imposed racial segregation. It was the encapsulated world of my childhood and youth. The only world I knew then, a world of senses which seeped into my consciousness transforming me in subtle ways, turning me into the man I have become. It took me a long while to understand, to realise that there was another world just over the horizon.

Certainly, my immediate family-life contributed much to my identity, influencing my values, habits of mind, looks and preferences. To this day, I fancy cooking curries the way my mother did. I can still conjure up the image of her deftly removing from the oven of her sturdy black coal stove a fresh-baked oval-shaped bread. The distinct yeasty aroma was irresistible.

Now almost eighty years on, I realise that the dividing line between reality and memory, between memory and imagination may be rather tenuous. As I write, the textured tapestry of the 1940s and 50s Cato Manor unfolds in my mind's eye.

I spot a stork or two dropping, long legs extended, onto a patch of fresh-ploughed field. One moves its neck snake-like and strikes, catching a cricket. Its companion stands still on one leg like a Masai herdsman. It was common knowledge that these precious white birds migrated each summer all the way from Holland where they built their nests of straw near chimney pots. I have not seen a single stork since those early years. There were also the brown long-tailed birds (we called them slazis) which often beat us to a ripened pawpaw, creating gaping holes. This silly bird, so engrossed in making a meal of the fruit, would often be oblivious to us wicked boys creeping up with catapults. What a 'pot shot' it made! The myna birds, I recall, were prolific and noisy. It did not please me that they were called *Indian* mynas since it seemed to demean the image of the Indian.

Slender pawpaw trees grew in most back gardens. Indian South Africans loved growing fruit trees anywhere on their modest allotments – front, back or sides of their houses. It was almost second nature for us to know the more common fruit trees by name: mango, guava, avocado, lemon, banana. Jackfruit trees were huge, and so were the fruit whose outer casing reminded me of an armadillo carapace. There was a jackfruit tree at my maternal grandparents' house in Aryan Road. Once, when I was there on a sleep-over, I was jolted in mid-sleep by a crashing sound in the backyard, like a large sack of potatoes falling off a vegetable delivery van. The mighty fall would split open the casing to reveal a feast of yellow fleshy segments. The sweetish smell of an overripe jackfruit was overpowering. Eating it was messy with our hands soon covered with a resin-like substance, which we would remove with cooking oil. It is most likely that most of the fruit here originated in India.

'What's so special about your fruit?' a fellow Australian neighbour once asked, 'I've bought and eaten local and imported avocados, paw paws, guavas and mangos often, and they've tasted just fine.' I protested with vehemence. 'No, no. Believe me. The fruits grown in Durban are totally different and much tastier.' Of course, my friend simply humoured me. 'Yeh, yeh, too right.' He would probably never claim to have seen or heard of mutton goolas (Natal Plum) – a dense shrub with vicious thorns that produced glorious reddish pink fruit. For some reason, the ripest fruit would be enticingly out of reach, ensconced in the thorny dark and glossy foliage. You would almost hear it teasing, 'Come get me - if you can.'

Summers were always hot and sticky. Very tropical. As a teenager, I always worried my armpits smelt. Of an afternoon at school or at a soccer match, I would glance repeatedly at the darkening sky, growing ever more anxious of being caught in a lightning storm as I ran home This wasn't needless fretting, but fear born of a traumatic experience. I recall once, when I would have been about twelve, running home *shit scared* (as the expression goes), all the way from the football field next to the Cato Manor cemetery as lightening cracked its vicious whip all about me. I cried and whimpered '*Arjuna, Arjuna, Arjuna,*' pleading to the Indian god of thunder to be merciful and spare me. My mother, wide-eyed, opened the front door against the determined wind. I fell into her embrace drenched and numb with terror.

After a brief storm, the world would appear steamy and refreshed. The afternoon sun would reassert itself. Rain birds (swallows) would be out in force crisscrossing the sky deftly devouring *easels* (flying ants) in mid-air, as wave after wave of these insects flapped their wings in a desperate attempt to escape the onslaught. They had shed their wings and fallen to the ground hoping to scurry into a dark place, but only to be devoured by waiting predators like frogs and lizards.

The names of many common flowering plants and shrubs of my early years are etched in my memory, infused with the all too familiar landscapes of home. On my way to the bus stop or school, I would spot clumps of colourful flowering trees and bushes - poinsettia, pride of India, hibiscus, and bougainvillea with their flower-spangled arms reaching over fences. Vacant lots and untended back yards would be thick with bush, briars and creepers all gone wild and carefree. The purple blue morning glory would cover bush and shrubs with indiscriminate glee. Just about visible under this cover, would be the fleshy leaves of sisal with spikes at the pointy ends, and dusky broad-leafed bush tobacco. I also came to recognize the *kaffir boom*, a tree native to this area. It had a sparse leaf-cover but was made up with bunches of attractive small trumpet-shaped orange-red flowers. I had seen cows rub themselves against the trunk of the *kaffir boom* as the bark was coarser than elephant hide.

People were generally a little wary of the elegant oleander shrub with pink and white flowers. Children were warned that these were haunted trees. I had seen many at the Cato Manor cemetery and crematorium, where my mother years later would be buried (and forgotten over time by family, including me). Perhaps the oleander flourish here because of the deep red earth fertilized by the countless burials of garden-loving, *green-fingered* Indians. I later learnt that all parts of the tree were toxic, and people ingesting the leaves or flowers were known to become deranged. Yet resourceful wayward boys discovered that the branches of the oleander provided the sturdiest Y-shaped handles for catapults.

The syringa was quite common. Always seen laden with perfumed bloom or full of yellow berries bunched like grapes. The bitter leaves were considered by my family to have medicinal properties. I have a vivid picture of grandmother repeatedly smearing a yellow wet paste of syringa leaves and turmeric on the entire body of Uncle Sunny (my mother's younger brother) when, soon after returning from war in Egypt, he came down with a most virulent form of measles. We cried believing he would soon die as doctors couldn't do much for him. But in a fortnight of treatment with grandmother's powerful potion, my uncle began to stir. The turmeric and syringa paste fell off his body like parchment, revealing healthy healing skin. Uncle lived a long life but turned out to be the most surly and mean-spirited person I had ever known. Could it have been the unavoidable side-effect of grandmother's miracle paste?

Greater Durban is mostly a landscape of hills and river valleys. But in the Cato Manor of my childhood, there were also treacherous gravel roads hemmed by drains and *dongas* (gullies formed by heavy rain). I recall occasions of disastrous floods when even minor streams came down in a spate washing away people, houses, pets, and gardens. When the water flowed over the concrete bridge across the Cato Manor River, boys would play *dare* by wading through shin-deep water, dangling school shoes in their hands. Auntie, my mother's sister, would have me firmly by the hand as we stood on a ridge overlooking the bridge. 'Arreh,' she would exclaim with fingers on her lip, 'look at the boys. They've no sense doing a risky thing like that.'

The Cato Manor River skirted Bellair Road, the main road for traffic from town. Rickety buses owned by relatively wealthy Indian entrepreneurs, plied this road. The buses were painted in garish primary colours, and had flamboyant names embossed on the sides and rear. One such inspired name was *Kunthi's Dream* (Kunthi, I'd guess, was the name of the bus owner's wife or daughter, or less likely the mother, and even less likely a favourite grandmother).

The hurtling buses and cars would make a momentary squelching noise as they sped by the all-and-sundry CN Rana's Shop, reducing to pulp and string the sisal leaves strewn on the road on purpose by the ingenious workers of the store. Once shredded and dry, the lengths of sisal fibre were collected and used as rope to tie up small bundles of firewood for sale.

Pedestrians on the way to CN Rana's were wary when walking this stretch of Bellair Road. Many a time, from my grandparents' wood and iron house, I'd see people screaming and scattering. I would laugh thinking it rather funny, but my irate grandfather pinched my ear one day. 'It's funny, eh? Wait till a bee stings you, my boy. Now go inside before I whack you.' Only later was I told bees nested in the cliff-face along Bellair Road. In periodic fits of rage, they would attack innocent passers-by. Thereafter, whenever my eyes strayed to the cliff-face, I would imagine spotting swarms taking off to wage war on people - especially market gardeners for indiscriminate clearing and burning of their habitats of wildflower.

Burning rubbish and garden clearings was quite common. Patches of mealie stalks were to be seen long after harvest time paper-dry and spent, waiting to be cut down and disposed of. I can remember plumes of grey acrid smoke rising into the late autumn sky, swaying, and drifting in the gentle breeze.

At about the age of ten, I moved with my family to a house of our own nearby in Mayville. Ronnie Govender's sketch map in his book *At the Edge and Other Cato Manor Stories* (1996), shows Mayville as just a newer part of Cato Manor. A brisk walk of about fifty minutes would get my father from our new house in Mayville to the previous rented one in Cato Manor. But the landscape in which I now moved and breathed seemed subtly different. Of course, I was a little older and more aware of my surroundings and allowed to venture out and explore with minimal supervision. When sent to buy the daily loaf of Baker's bread and a bottle of Clover Dairy milk, it proved the ideal opportunity to wander. 'Why so late again, eh?' my mother would admonish. 'Just to Udyian's so long time, eh? Wait till your father comes home.'

Often, when seated at the table in the dining room doing homework, I would allow my eyes to stray through the open door, to scan the already familiar landscape in the near distance: Bellair Road with frantic traffic going both ways, and Mayville Theatre, where I had seen many a cowboy movie immediately after school, unbeknown to my parents. Eightpence was what I would pay to enter. The land behind the cinema rose to a respectable hill covered in grass and thicket. That is where we would go on our secret picnics, two or three special classmates and me. We would pool what little pocket money we had to buy half a loaf of brown (whole meal) bread, a tin of Glenryck pilchards in tomato sauce, and an onion. What a memorable picnic feast that made. My fingers would smell of tinned fish and onions long after I returned home – which was always a give-away worry.

We lived on the slopes of a hill in Mayville, crowded with ramshackle houses of Indian families. It descended into a valley along which ran Standard Road, following the course of a shallow sickly stream. My house sat in the middle of a grid of roads forming a rectangle – Standard Road at the bottom, Jansen's Avenue on the top, and Rathlin and Droma Roads on either side. A network of other roads stretched out on all sides from these four roads. Familiar landmarks that dotted across the network became signposts by which we navigated or gave others direction much like how songs embedded with markers of landscape served the indigenous peoples in the Australian outback. This was our grounded territory, our internalised landscape which defined the immediate lives of the people of Cato Manor.

When Indian families were evicted from Cato Manor to make way for Whites under Apartheid, this familiar cultural landscape was systematically obliterated. Families and immediate neighbours were scattered, shunted to undeveloped fringes of Durban. My family settled in Reservoir Hills, hilly, rock-strewn and mostly yellow clay. It sat above the Umgeni River which flowed across a fertile valley, Springfield Flats. This river entered the sea at Blue Lagoon, a popular fishing spot, and not too far from where the frantic sardine shoals beached themselves annually. Poorer Indians developed thriving market gardens along the riverbanks. A cluster of shacks sprang up nearby with the euphemistic name Tin Town which was subject to regular flooding whenever the Umgeni River broke its banks.

I got to know new Indian neighbourhoods along the Umgeni River such as Sea Cow Lake, Newlands and Parlock. It was surprising how rapidly these areas acquired an intangible Indianness about them, almost as if the distinct smell of curry clung to the landscape.

The designated areas for black South Africans in this part of Durban such as Clermont and KwaMashu were far removed and largely remote and invisible from where Indians lived.

All this once seemingly solid terrain is now transformed – parts quite unrecognisable to me. The reality is that landscapes are not static. They are ever changing, becoming something else. And simultaneously re-imagined. Every moment in Cato Manor, it seems, was for me a passage of no return. Erased by time, relentless forces of change, politics, poverty, and population growth. It exists now only as a mindscape relegated to memory and captured in the imagined hand-sketched map of Ronnie Govender.

But there is one landmark of my childhood that has endured looming large above the waters of the bay – the Durban Bluff. It was certainly there when I returned by sea on 5 September 1969 from India after a few years of self-imposed absence abroad. I could not rejoice then in seeing it once more, brooding under a dark overcast sky. Far from rejoicing, I felt a foreboding not knowing what fearful challenges Apartheid had in store for me.

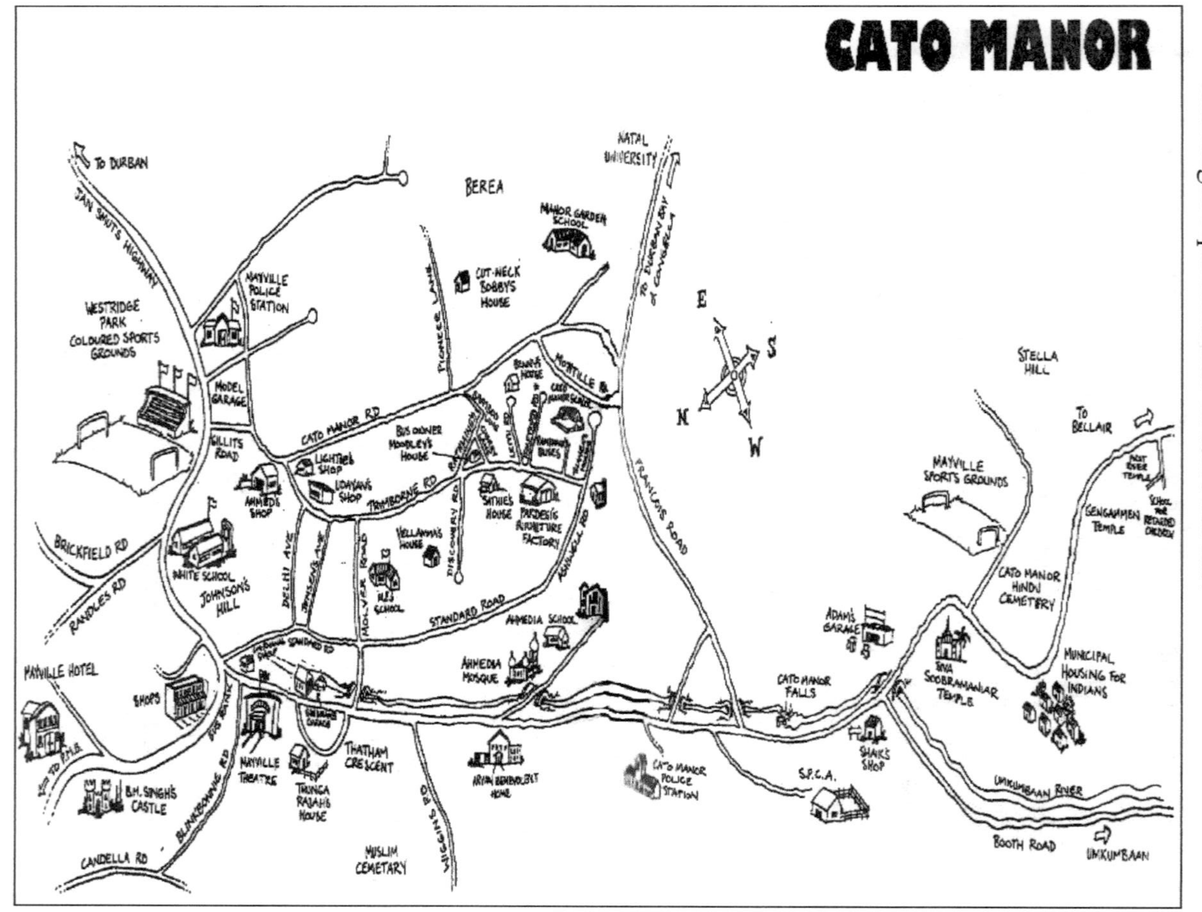

A Life Lived in South African Books and Writing

As much as my evolving identity was embedded in and shaped by the landscape of my early years, my growing interest and absorption in books also played a formative role in nurturing my expanding awareness of myself and the world about me. Reading drew me into alternative realities and possibilities. Got me thinking, comparing, and questioning. Feeding my imagination, introducing me to time travel.

~

During my primary school years (1946-54), the only story books we had at home were my mother's two Tamil readers published in India. They were slim volumes with discoloured pages. One was a book of devotional songs, and the other an introductory Tamil reader for children. This was not unusual at the time as few in my community would have had the financial means to invest in books. I had not even heard of such places as bookshops or libraries.

I was quite surprised to learn one day that there was a public library in Durban. We were on a class outing to the Durban Museum when the library was pointed out to us. It was located on a floor below the Museum, both housed in the old and distinguished Victorian-era City Hall. But this library was for the exclusive use of Europeans. A 'Whites Only' sign at the entrance warned us to take note. By now, most of us kids were quite accustomed to seeing such signs and understood their meaning.

Around 1950, the all-white Durban City Council, under pressure from non-white ratepayers, established the segregated Brook Street Library for non-whites in the town centre close to busy markets and bustling bus ranks. A longish unused railway shed, not too far from the Berea Station, was converted to serve this purpose. It would take me about forty minutes to get to the library by bus from Cato Manor where we lived.

I was about thirteen years old when my father enrolled me as a member, but only after I had pestered my mother for weeks. I felt overjoyed and special while holding my borrower's card, knowing that none in my family seemed interested in reading, apart from the daily evening paper. I cannot recall any of my neighbours or school friends borrowing books either. I visited the library on Saturday mornings after my father and I had done the shopping. I would make sure to carry my library book in my hand for everyone to see. My pride as a reader knew no bounds.

Although I continued to be an avid reader into my youth, I have little recollection of what captured my fancy at that time – romance, boys' adventures, crime? I do, however, recall becoming immersed in comics especially Superman, Batman & Robin, American war comics obsessing about the yellow peril (China) and, much later, Classic Comics which featured stories of novelists like Mark Twain, Charles

Dickens, and Jules Verne. These I bought by penny-pinching whenever I was sent to the corner Tea Room for bread, milk, and newspapers.

Late into my high school years, I stumbled upon English stories set in South Africa, distinguishing these from foreign ones such as Shakespeare, Dickens and the like introduced to us in school.

Some books from my youth and early adulthood have left lasting impressions, books that would likely have fed my imagination and influenced how I saw the world.

A few discoloured and tattered books still sit snugly on the top-most shelf in my study in Melbourne as clues to my early reading choices. My attachment to them is pure sentiment. These books have travelled with me whenever my family moved. Eventually they *migrated* with me to Australia.

To start with, there are two books once considered classics in South Africa. Whether they still hold this venerated appeal, I have no idea.

The first is Percy FitzPatrick's *Jock of the Bushveld* published in 1907. It is a story of a bull terrier and his owner, a transport rider in the early gold rush days in South Africa. I recall, as a teenager still in shorts, finding a quiet corner of the house to hide from family and, undisturbed, pore over the gripping adventures of Jock, a bold and plucky little dog, his coat the colour of burnished gold. Over the course of the story, Jock survived several dangerous encounters. However, his luck ran out one evening when he was set upon by marauding dogs as he stood his ground protecting his master's chicken coop.

I was simply distraught when the novel ended with Jock being found fatally wounded. The image conjured up in my mind was too painful and traumatic. Jock died cradled in his master's arms as the first miraculous life-affirming sunlight broke over the *veld*, the expansive grassland of the high country. And such finality in the concluding sentence. *Jock had done his duty*. I sobbed, too distressed (and naive) to accept the reality of death. Why, oh why did Jock have to die? The world was a most cruel place if goodness could perish in this way. I sulked over many days to the puzzled concern of my mother.

The last pencil sketch in the book was of Jock trotting happily along a dirt track, into the soft glow of an autumn sunset.

~

The second book is Herman Charles Bosman's collection *Mafeking Road and Other Stories,* first published in 1947. The stories of Bosman captivated me after I attended a stage reading. The reader was Patrick Mynhardt, an accomplished actor, who had mastered Bosman's stories. He was large and sturdy, wore a beard, and had a bemused face with a perpetual twinkle in his eyes. This was how Mynhardt chose to portray the narrator of Bosman's stories, Oom Schalk Lourens, a wily rustic character who had a sharp eye and a wry ironic insight into his community. Mynhardt's voice was a sonorous rumble like distant thunder.

Of course, I assumed that the persona of the actor on stage was one and the same as the narrator created by Bosman. A bearded, wise old Dutch farmer sitting on a stool at a cosy fireplace in the kitchen, smoking a pipe and weaving all these whimsical stories in his head to amuse and confound his listeners.

The backdrop of *Mafeking Road* is the remote Groot Marico, a rural Afrikaner village (dorp) in the northern bushlands of the Transvaal, where marauding wild animals were still to be found. It was a time when the Boers were warring with both the British (Rooineks) and local indigenous tribes referred to as *Kaffirs* at that time. Horses and carts were the means of transport. The Boer community were mostly illiterate, poor, god-fearing racists. Hence, for me Bosman painted a picture of a world both intriguing and very foreign, much like the setting of fairy tales. Stories that unfolded with a dream-like quality and often quite funny. Oom Schalk Lourens entertained his listeners in foolish, weird, or eccentric tales, making them sound convincing, true to rural life. Like fables, these stories conveyed a moral.

As a young avid reader, it did not seem to matter to me that the stories were about Afrikaners, white people who disliked us. This thought may have come to me much later. But the truth is that even to this day I enjoy Bosman's writing as literature that is authentic and original, of a bygone era. And they are not unlike the stories of early Australian writers such as Henry Lawson and Banjo Paterson.

My political awakening happened gradually as I moved from high school years (1955-58) into university life. I discovered and became drawn to books, fiction, and non-fiction, with themes of race, colour, and political oppression. By now I was becoming aware of the political and racial tensions all around me, the hardships suffered by the oppressed in South Africa, and personally felt the bitter taste of abuse. I began to be angered and roused by daily harsh actions of the all-white government and the police. It soon dawned upon me that I was not just an Indian but part of a larger non-white population. I had no choice but to attend a non-white university. There was a subtle shift in the books I began reading.

One of the books from this era that is still in my collection is Olive Schreiner's *The Story of an African Farm,* first published in 1883. The backdrop was a rugged, wind-swept part of South Africa called the Eastern Cape. The story took place in colonial times during the reign of Queen Victoria. A sparse and unrelenting rural landscape accentuated the prevailing themes of impoverishment, racial discrimination, and exploitation of women. Olive Schreiner was a free spirit and a suffragette. A woman ahead of her time.

This autobiographical novel, first published in 1883, was an easy read. However, I am almost certain that the subtleties of the themes would have eluded me as a non-white teenager growing up under Apartheid. What resonated and has remained with me all these years are a few fragmentary images. One was of the protagonist, Waldo, worn out by age, loneliness, and poverty squatting on his haunches in the warmth of the morning sun, his arms folded and resting on his knees. He was so motionless that a chicken, pecking at the dry earth, pecked at his boots without the least fear. They knew better. Waldo, the stoic man, had finally departed, leaving behind an unfulfilled life of desolation and pain. Here again, the finality of death was what haunted me long after I had shut the book. The irony, however, was that in identifying with Waldo and his stoic suffering, I had really thought I was investing my compassion on an oppressed and dispossessed black man – or at least a person of mixed parentage (Coloured). Now belatedly, I have discovered that Waldo was in fact of German descent.

I am not exactly sure how I stumbled upon Peter Abrahams, a gifted South African writer of coloured background. It could have been in my high school years when I perhaps became a more discerning user of the Brook Street Library, and when I was becoming increasingly aware of the politics of the time. It is likely, too, that the tantalizing titles of Abrahams' books caught my attention: *Tell Freedom, Return to Goli, Dark Testament, Mine Boy, A Wreath for Udomo, The Path of Thunder, Wild Conquest.*

Reading *Mine Boy* (1946) opened my eyes, in a disturbing and telling way, to the plight and suffering of ordinary, impoverished Blacks. It affected me more profoundly than when I had seen black people harassed by police not too far from the Brook Street Library. Abraham's relatively short simply written novel speaks of the exploited and soulless life of a black migrant worker who leaves his family behind in some distant rural village to work in the gold mines on the Witwatersrand. He suffers great indignity living in a congested filthy dormitory with countless other black men, his bed as his only personal space.

I realise now that Peter Abrahams was the very first non-white writer to come my way, and his books were profoundly absorbing. The emotional impact of *Mine Boy* would linger long after I'd come to the end and closed the book – and I had moved onto another good book.

Alan Paton's *Cry, the Beloved Country*, published in

1948, became an internationally acclaimed classic. The theme of the novel was the corrosive tensions existing between rural and urban lives, effectively between black and white communities in South Africa. This was a time when the unwelcome impact of a white-driven moneyed economy caused traditional rural family life to unravel. Young disaffected black men resorted to crime as the surest way to get their share of conspicuous material wealth. Paton's story explored the profound and painful repercussions when a black youth from a strong Christian background murdered a young white man whose parents too were ardent Christians. It was not just any white man, but a passionate liberal who was on a mission to fight for the social betterment of Blacks. Nowadays, Blacks would feel strongly against this theme as being no more than blatant old-fashioned white Christian patronage – the view that the interests of poor Blacks could best be represented by *liberal* Whites. In the story the murderer was repentant, seeking forgiveness, and was redeemed.

I recall the evocative landscape with which the novel opens, deliberately casting into relief the appalling crime. We read passages of the book in high school, and I recall how Paton used lyrical writing to accentuate the pathos of the story.

Paton was often in the news, and I attended political meetings where he spoke as the founder and leader of the South African Liberal Party. He was a short stocky man, with a strong jaw line and a fierce clipped manner of speaking. He would stare at the audience with his piercing eyes from over his glasses that hung low on his nose. He may have been himself a passionate Christian.

Fifty years on, in 1998, Sindiwe Magona, an accomplished black female writer, had her novel *Mother to Mother* published. Ever since, it has been a prescribed reader in high schools. I came upon it when I visited South Africa in 2018. What amazed me was how closely Magona's story and theme resembled Alan Paton's book. Here, a black mother discovers her son has joined a mob of black youth who set upon a young unsuspecting white girl, a foreign student, when she strayed into their township to drop off a fellow black student. She was bludgeoned to death in a frenzy of anti-white rage. The distraught mother of the boy reached out to the traumatized mother of the murdered girl pleading for her to understand how generations of living under colonial-era discrimination followed by Apartheid had fractured black family life and had virtually eroded the capacity of parents to rear and nurture children. Consequently, boys in the black ghettos had become brutalized, developing a vengeful hatred of Whites. While the mother of the boy pleaded to high heaven for her son's forgiveness, she resigned herself to the reality of crime and punishment. Her sorrow for the mother of the murdered girl ran deep, yet not even an ocean of grieving could set things right. I had the sense that the gods were either not listening or felt powerless in the face of man's inherent inhumanity to man. The stuff of an ancient Greek tragedy.

My interest in theatre initially arose from my three-year study of speech and drama at Natal University. This opened my eyes to how alive theatre was at the time, especially protest theatre, a vogue in the sixties and seventies. Here the focus was themes of political and social inequities under Apartheid. This was experimental theatre – at times quite amateurish and didactic – with little evidence of the subtleties of stage craft. I kept an eye on what was being staged, where, who the producer was, and the performers. And I attempted to attend as many performances as possible. My interest in protest–theatre related to my involvement at the time in struggle-politics. For a time, an added incentive was a commission I had from *The Graphic* (Indian) weekly to write short theatre reviews. I was usually given two free tickets to shows. Transport to the venues in the city and back home at night was a perennial challenge.

~

The playwright, Athol Fugard, together with his two leading black male actors, Winston Ntshona and John Kani, became all too familiar. Although they based themselves mostly at the now famous Market Theatre in Johannesburg, their shows invariably staged in Durban as well. These three, in their self-effacing humble appearance, were to me so much alike. They were near middle-age, short and stocky, and every bit working class. Their plays confronted issues of social inequality and racial oppression as experienced by the dispossessed masses. They were mostly staged in fringe venues accessible to non-whites. However, the performances were equally well supported and acclaimed by affluent and educated liberal Whites and the English-language press. Of course, the shows also received close attention from the security police.

The titles of three of Fugard's plays are etched in my mind as they depicted in vivid images and anguished voices the fractured lives of impoverished and dispossessed people in South Africa under Apartheid. Themes of compassion and humanity are central in *Sizwe Banzi is Dead, Blood Knot,* and *Boesman and Lena.* I regret not possessing copies of these plays.

I also recall seeing the movie *Tsotsi* based on Fugards's 2006 novel of the same name. Yet again the agonizing theme differed only slightly from that of Paton and Mangona in their novels. 'See,' Fugard seems to be saying, 'the pernicious harm Apartheid has wrought upon black youth, turning them into vicious mindless thugs who spare no one, not even their own kind.'

Besides these authors, I also became familiar with works of South African Indian playwrights Kessie Govender, Ronnie Govender and Strini Moodley. Kessie founded the Stable Theatre in Durban where he staged protest plays such as *Working-class Hero* and *the Shack.* Ronnie's plays had a more satirical edge to them. As I recall, the plays were commentaries on the political machinations, affiliations, and tensions in the Indian community. The audience at these performances was predominantly Indian. For me, his collection of short stories (*At the Edge and Other Cato Manor Stories,* 1996) had a greater appeal. They related to a life familiar to me and as lived by Indians in Cato Manor in the fifties, before they were uprooted under the Group Areas Act. The stories brought alive the world I'd known intimately. As a young boy, Cato Manor was my home ground. *At the Edge* has been performed on stage at several international theatre festivals, to much acclaim.

However, Strini Moodley was relatively more

confrontational as he actively adopted theatre to advance the ideology of the Black Consciousness Movement, very current at the time. I have a vivid mental picture of him on stage – tall, dark, and strident. He would be joined in his plays by notable others such as Asha Rambally, Saths Cooper and Sam Moodley. It is a pity I can't seem to recall the titles of plays they wrote, adapted, or improvised. They also engaged in protest verse and narrative monologues which encouraged the audience to be resolute in resisting oppression and being self-reliant as Blacks. Community theatre in its essence. The exhortations would be explicit, defiant, and uncompromising, even though the players were aware of the likely presence of security police in the audience taking note of every gesture and utterance. Strini was charged and sentenced for terrorism and served five years on Robben Island as a political prisoner with Mandela and other struggle stalwarts.

I'd got to know Strini quite well as he was my contemporary, and our paths often crossed –notably because I was also at the time taken up with the Black Consciousness inspired South African Students Association (SASO) led by Steve Biko. Further, Strini's father, Mr NG Moodley, was my boss when I was employed at Lakehaven Children's Home.

Many books were banned under Apartheid. The government's censorship board was overzealous in readily labelling what it disliked as communist propaganda and a threat to the state. At one time I heard that the classic children's novel *Black Beauty* by Anna Sewell was banned because of the words black and beuty in the title.

I recall the mixed feelings of fear and daring when I read and passed on banned books. I soon became skilled in furtive

124

whispering and clandestine sharing of politically charged literature such as: *Soul on Ice* by Eldridge Cleaver (1968); The *Autobiography of Malcolm X* (1965); *The Fire Next Time* by James Baldwin (1963); *Mao's Red Book* (1964); *Time Longer than Rope* by Edward Roux (1948). On occasions, I stumbled upon copies of *Sechaba*, the magazine of the armed wing of the African National Congress in exile (published across the South African border). I knew that I would receive a very harsh sentence for possessing or transmitting so-called seditious literature. But this did not seem to deter me. Once when the security police raided my family home, it was my brother who had the presence of mind to throw two of my banned books out the bedroom window.

In the mid-1950s and into the '60s there was a renaissance of young black writer-journalists. I found them by way of the *Drum Magazine* and the related literary journal *The Classic*. I became intoxicated with such names as Can Themba, Nat Nakasa, Todd Matshikiza, Lewis Nkosi, Bloke Modisane and Casey Motsisi – the so-called 'Drum Boys.' They were talented in the use of English. It seems it was a time of rapid change, turmoil, and uncertainty – and excitement. They lived at the edge, drinking, womanizing, taking enormous risks in venturing out to report on crime, poverty, police brutality and so on, as if they had an instinctive sense that their charmed lives would not last. In my collection of valued pamphlets, magazines, and newspaper clippings of that heady period, I find just a single copy of *The Classic*. In a decade *Drum* lost its steam (after having become the most read magazine in Africa), the cream of the journalists and photographers had scattered. Nat

Nakasa exiled himself to the USA, only to find isolation and the loss of home unbearable. He committed suicide by jumping from a high-rise apartment in New York in 1965 at the age of 28. He had been the first editor of *The Classic* magazine.

The Heinemann African Writers Series burst upon the literary world in 1962 with Chinua Achebe as the founding editor. Within a few years, there were almost a hundred titles published of quality and original African writing. Some of the South African writers on this list were Dennis Brutus, Alex La Guma, Nelson Mandela and Can Themba. The distinct orange and white cover with black print caught my attention like a magnet whenever I visited the library or grazed in a bookshop. Of course, the very first book I read in this series was Achebe's now classic *Things Fall Apart* (1958).

My deep interest in South African literature has continued to this day. If anything, I feel I have become more discerning and selective of what I read. I am conscious of the limited hours remaining in my twilight years. However, Damon Galgut continues to be one of my favourite novelists.

Sadly, here in Australia I feel cut-off and isolated from the on-the-ground vibrancy of the literary buzz in South Africa. At the same time, I am quite uninformed of the lay readership in South Africa who may be reminiscing about the writing world that I had lived through. Would there be many who continue to marvel at all the inspirational writers who had gone before, celebrate the literature that captured life as it was then, particularly for the oppressed and dispossessed masses? Or is this interest relegated to academia?

I concede, too, I retain in my mind little of the substance

of that literature. There is a subdued thrill in recognizing and roll-calling the names of these writers even as they inevitably vanish into the gloom of dusk. I wish I had the time and energy to revisit this literature if only to remind me of the crazy impassioned world in which they lived, loved, and captured in such imaginative writing. But that's no more than wishful sentiment. Even the thoughts I record here and share with you have a dubious and limited shelf life. All is of equal value - all grist to the mill. As Marcel Proust, a renowned French writer of the nineteenth century, muses: 'No doubt my books too, like my fleshy being, would in the end one day die....... A self in me deplores the loss of these treasures, (but) then I perceive that memory, as it withdraws from me, carries away with it this self too.' (*In Search of Lost Time,* 1996),

~

Looking back now, there is no doubt in my mind that books and reading enabled me to learn about South Africans who existed beyond my narrow ethnic horizon, to know them as people not unlike me and my family. They, too, in various ways experienced a mix of joys and struggle, loss and perhaps lasting pain. And there was endurance, too, through sheer courage. This I found uplifting. In such moments, I felt at one with them, forgetting barriers of race, colour, or creed. My pukka *Indianness* may have begun dissolving then, in favour of a *South Africanness.*

~

The opportunity to read widely also raised my political awareness, accentuated my sense of disadvantage, and got me thinking about what would make for a better country, and

ways in which disaffected people could aspire to transcend
barriers imposed by racial prejudice and Apartheid.

Homecoming

Tribute to returning exiles.
(Published in *Staffrider* V9, N4 1991)

Our individual and collective glory
Sung,
We lay down our arms.
Recede into the mass of
Faceless braves
(Comrades all!).

Past days of anguished pain,
Relentless memories of exile
In foreign lands!
(We never believed it possible),
Overlaid
By new pain, new uncertainties.

Comrades all,
Exiles in a strange land
Our Motherland!
Presenting a brave face
Harmonising together a different song:
'Happy days are here again...'

Covid Essays

Undone by Covid

Covid is an inconsiderate bastard. Working from home and stuck to my desk, I become oblivious to the passage of time and day. Such a blur.

'Are you here? Cannn't seeee ya.' Belinda's voice message sounded playful, but barely conceals her irritation. And she should be. After all, I was to have met her at Murrumbeena Park almost 15 minutes ago. 'Sorry,' I messaged back. 'Caught up; will be there in 10 minutes.'

She and I were long time workmates. We both opted to work from home, safe and cloistered from the risk of Covid. We used to catch up regularly, but rarely ever now. Belinda is fastidious about 'not taking risks.' And super-anxious about bugs. I recall once at work telling her in passing that I felt a cold coming on. A bit of a sore throat. Just that, and she recoiled with visible horror. *Keep away, keep awa,y I don't want it*. I felt quite put off. Really did.

But now she's the one who initiated this unexpected catchup after a lapse of a year – as if she's wanting to *test the water*. 'What if we met in the open at Murrumbeena Park?' she suggested. No problem, I had replied agreeing on a time and date.

As I hastened to strip off my *trackies* and get into something decent, I realised with mild alarm that my wife had gone to the doctors with my car. Shit! Can't wait for her to return, bloody well have to drive the Subaru now.

I've always been oddly nervous about the Subaru. It seemed as bulky as a *buffalo* compared to my modest VW Beetle. At most, I've only managed reversing it out the driveway and parking it at the kerb. Now, all hurried and flustered, I pull it out the driveway into the road, checking and rechecking not to hit someone or something, all the while talking to myself. *You're okay. Easy does it. Almost there.*

As I near Murrumbeena Park, I check anxiously for a decent parking space along the street. Can't keep Belinda waiting much longer. But not much luck. Cars are lined up bumper to bumper on either side of the road. I continue driving slowing past the park while glancing anxiously at my rear-view mirror. Ah, there's a car just pulling out. Will have to make a quick U-turn before someone else grabs the spot. Traffic stalled ahead and behind, waiting patiently. I succeed. But I get out only to find that I'd parked miles from the kerb. I convinced myself that it was *good enough.*

I hasten to the pre-arranged meeting spot near the jungle gym and flying fox. But no Belinda. Where could she be? Better phone her, I think. Blast the buffeting winds and the cacophony of kids. I hadn't anticipated it would be so gusty or crowded. Not conducive for a quiet chat. With my partial hearing and the wind crackling, I don't quite grasp Belinda's response.

I try her from a different spot. *What? What?* No luck. But

then I get a further text. *I'm walking around the oval but don't see you.* Waiting for me at the other end, near the oval? What's wrong with her? Did I not text her with explicit directions where to meet? I hear the irritation deep in me. I phone her at once and gently reminded her of our arrangement. *Ay ha,* she says seemingly unruffled. *Okay then.* She offered to walk over from the oval end to meet me.

I keep my eye peeled as kids and minders crossing before me. In the meantime, the wind whips my overgrown hair from all sides. Hadn't had a haircut in two months because of lockdown.

I spot a largish woman walking toward me. She's masked and wearing a floppy wide-brimmed sun hat and wearing a loose-fitting floral Punjabi pants. I stare discreetly. Could it be my workmate?

'Hello,' she calls out. Goodness, it is her!

'I know, I know, you wouldn't make me out, right?' She laughed heartily.

'Sorry,' I say a little embarrassed. 'People behind their masks are a problem for me. Can't make them out.' But the reality was that I'd forgotten that she and I were both *seniors* now – and the aging process had simply kept apace under lockdown, away from my gaze.

Soon we're seated at a picnic table across from each other. There were a few more such tables close to a BBQ stand, but no takers. We chatted about this and that, but Belinda mostly spoke of frustration and stress with her tele-counselling work – lackadaisical clients who don't even phone to cancel appointments and the pressure from her team leader to be more productive as her monthly stats were far too low.

To change the subject, I happily told her about my excursion to Chadstone the day before to buy a book, only to find, to my utter surprise and annoyance, that most stores (including Kmart and Targets) were closed. I added that on returning home my wife had berated me. Hadn't I heard on the radio, she had shouted, that Chadstone was declared a 'hotspot' that very morning!

My aborted trip to Chadstone didn't seem to amuse Belinda. She removed her gaudy hat, momentarily exposing her trademark fiery tinted shoulder-length hair and ran her fingers through it. But the gusts of wind promptly lifted and ruffled the hair exposing the greying of age.

Only much later did I realise that my story may have rung alarm bells for Belinda. What if I had caught the virus! And the wind dispersed it her way. How thoughtless of me. We parted abruptly without ceremony. That was the last I saw of her. I have since given up work.

Covid Mind Games

Melbourne, voted the world's most liveable city, is facing Stage 4 lockdown from midnight. How bloody awful. The Premier announced the news looking grave and severe, like a grandfather barely coping with ill-disciplined grandkids. 'I'm sorry, but because some thoughtless people ignored my stay safe message, all of you will now have to wear the additional pain.'

I went to bed fearful and frustrated. Tossed and turned much of the night, dozing only fitfully, troubled by a recurring nightmare. Alien capsules from outer space floated down from the night sky landing across the landscape. Each resembled a bloated red coronavirus, complete with deadly spikes. I feared they'd split open and let-loose octopus-like creatures programmed to syphon the breath out of earthlings. I tumbled out of bed, still drowsy and drained. Hey man, get real, I cautioned, or you'll go batty. Why let Covid rattle you!

~

The morning was shrouded in a gloomy wintry chill. I ought to get out and get some exercise, I thought, before I go bonkers shut in all day. Fresh air should do me good. Why waste my exercise hour, the daily outdoor freebee bestowed upon every citizen by the Premier!

Motivated, I set a steady pace along Corona Street. A large ginger cat suddenly appeared on the footpath ahead and ambled towards me. I paid it little attention. In my experience, any sensible cat will veer off with the approach of a human. But not this one. No, this ginger feline thing didn't bugger off, but rather sauntered nonchalantly closer and closer towards me. I felt a little bewildered, irritated, and vaguely uneasy. I slowed my pace, pretending not to notice. The cat almost brushed past with total indifference, without giving an inch. Staying its course, flouting the social distancing rule. I adjusted my facemask and glanced instinctively behind me, hoping to see the cat disappear into someone's property. But no, it didn't. The bloody thing stalled, confronting me on the footpath, staring fixedly with inscrutable menace. I quickened my pace, then broke into a run. I had a sudden urge to be safely home. Once through the gate, I yanked off my facemask, panting.

'You okay, dear?' inquired my wife, frowning with concern as she watered a pot-plant on the veranda.

I said nothing. Feeling foolish and heart pumping, I simply collapsed onto a garden bench and bent over to breathe easy, much relieved that my precious breath hadn't taken off to netherworld.

Wise Shakespeare cautioned that strange behaviours of birds and beast portended grave events in the affairs of men. I found myself uneasily glued to TV news and scanning newspapers for reports of strange and inscrutable happenings, for more sightings of prowling ginger cats,

Unmasked and Faceless

On any night in Melbourne, about three hundred homeless people may be found sleeping rough in the city streets, sweltering in summer, and freezing in winter.

Late one morning, I took a train into the city and walked along the crowded and popular Swanston Street from the Young and Jackson Pub to the State Library, a distance of no more than a kilometre and a half. I would have seen as many as five destitute adults occupying the pavements. I recall one man propped up against a shop front, shaggy head drooping onto his knees, his cap nearby with a few meagre coins. There was a woman (or a man, I couldn't tell for sure) under a worn grey blanket, wearing a beanie and deeply asleep. Her possessions included two well-worn plastic bags of stuff and a scrawny four-legged companion curled up close by. I also recall a youngish man dazed and unsteady, leaning against a pillar, his face weather-worn, unshaven, his eyes weepy. The man held up an appeal scrawled on a piece of cardboard: *Spare the man a feed?* I felt pained at the hopelessness of his gesture. A dark-complexioned old man in a wheelchair waved a magazine at passers-by. He caught my eye as he called out '*Big Issue. All the latest, Big Issue.*' A steady flow of self-absorbed shoppers and visitors walked briskly past, seemingly oblivious. Or did they simply avert their gaze from the homeless by choice?

Melbourne is touted as a *first world* city with a population of five million. It is the *place to be* for the healthy, wealthy, and young. A mecca for Asian students. When the Lord Mayor walks the streets with distinguished international visitors pointing out with evident pride the city's magnificent achievements, I wonder if she turns a practised blind eye on the destitute souls who stare her in the face. And does she hope that the tinted glasses of the visitors would filter out the unsavoury sights? It almost seems to me that the city authorities don't consider homelessness as a priority to be addressed, but rather an uncomfortable reality of life best shelved for now. However, the first wave of Covid-19 to hit Melbourne, caught the City Council and the State Government on the hop.

Suddenly, the homeless and destitute souls on the streets became a highly visible danger, a potential threat to the good health of Melbournians. The authorities hit the panic button. *Get them off the streets before they spread the virus around. Now, now! No time to waste! Quarantine them. If need be, lock them up in hotels.*

'Tell the government to piss off,' shouted an affronted man cloistered in a stairwell when a Red Cross volunteer arrived to escort him to a nearby hotel, with the media in tow. 'Bin sleepin rough me whole life, mate. Ya want me out and into a posh hotel for 14 days? Leave me swag behind? What for? How's that'll solve me need for reliable digs, eh? Chrissake, I don't need no isolation. I'm it now.'

He had a point. The once bustling city streets were ghostly still with nervous shoppers and visitors having taken flight.

The rather perplexed Red Cross volunteer stood his distance adjusting his mask as the man, his dignity ruffled, flung his hand about and ranted, 'Come Melbourne Cup, the city gets a mop and bucket treatment. Me, I get shunted to May's shelter. A flea pit, I tell ya. And fifteen pricks to a stinkin loo. Fuck it, I say and go AWOL. Pissing under the stars I feel liberated like. Yeah.'

A TV reporter turned up at the four-star Knox Hotel to see how the homeless were adjusting there. He spotted an oldish woman in the hotel foyer wearing crumpled over-sized jeans and looking quite lost and agitated. A weary-faced security guard was urging her to put on her facemask and return to her room. But he wasn't winning. She gave him a mouthful.

'Facemask? What bloody facemask, eh?'

A good moment to step in, thought the reporter. He thrust his microphone into her fuming face and quizzed her. 'Compared to street life, is this hotel comfy like Buckingham Palace, eh?'

The woman brushed aside the microphone and glared. 'I tell ya, this place's a shocker to me system,' she whispered in a smoker's voice. 'Dragged here like a mangy dog. Without bin asked.'

'But you must enjoy your room, surely?' persisted the naïve young man.

'Fancy-smelling pillows, and there's me staring back at myself from mirrors large as Father Christmas. Drives me nuts.'

Notwithstanding the drastic lockdown and large-scale

quarantine strategy, there's now palpable alarm that the pandemic may linger, that the current devastated economic life of the city will not rebound and, that it was virtual goodbye to cash generating international students. So much for the glitter, glamour, and much vaunted vibrancy of Melbourne. Anticipated wholesale job losses and unemployment will trigger mortgage failures and evictions from rental properties. And heaps more are likely to swell the ranks of those at the edge of homelessness.

Hanging Out in Times of Covid

The phone pings in my pocket. I pause in the midst of my morning walk to read the text: *Would you like to hang out this weekend?* It is my twentysomething Cambodian-Australian neighbour, Norris. Really? I think. Me an old man of eighty *hang out* with a spring chicken! Just picture it! Whatever could have prompted him, I wonder, amused, puzzled – and oddly uneasy.

Give him a break, I say to myself, simulating a sympathetic smile. It's a cultural thing, I guess. The poor bugger's not aware of the inappropriateness of his overture - and choice of words. He's also clearly forgotten the rules of Covid-19 lockdown.

Norris has been my neighbour for some three years. He lives with his parents. An only child. The couple in their late 50s don't speak English. They are contract cleaners and spend long hours away – leaving home early when it's still dark and returning at dusk. Sometimes I see the man mowing the front lawn and nature strip, and his wife tending to the vegetables she'd planted in a strip of tilled patch on the fringes of the lawn. When they spot me leaving for a walk, they raise their hands with a *Hi, ah ah,* accompanied with undecided and awkward smiles. But Norris speaks good English and has a friendly and respectful disposition. I suspect *Norris* is his adopted Aussie name. Probably his parents call him Chea, Sukun or something homely.

I've spoken to Norris intermittently over the three years, usually on my walks in the neighbourhood. He always seemed in haste. I'm puzzled.

On occasions, in the past, I've heard a mixed group of friends over the fence in cheerful party mood. But not since covid hit. Nor have I sighted Norris in months – so much so, that I wondered if he was away in Cambodia visiting family. Yet his car was always there in the front yard.

The last time we chatted was about six months ago. It was a gusty summer morning on a Sunday. I thought an early morning walk would be a good idea since a 35-degree day was predicted for Melbourne. If I go now, I'd thought, I'd detour via the Sunday Market on Hanover Street carpark. As I passed his house next door, Norris was rummaging into the boot of his car parked at the kerb. He noticed me and came over. We said hello and exchanged pleasantries, keeping our distance.

~

But let me return to the odd text I received from Norris while on my recent walk. It came when I was still adjusting to the surplus time on my hand – consequence of being housebound. I texted back, reminding him of the rules of lockdown but suggesting we may still catch up at my place - if that was okay with him. I say 2 pm on Sunday. He agreed.

I set out two stools on my veranda overlooking Bishop Street – two metres apart. Punctual myself, I plonk on

my stool with a copy of *The Age* and wait. A cool breeze
rustles in the giant Jacaranda tree in my front yard. Twenty
minutes lapses but no sign of my Cambodian friend. Mild
irritation. I phone him. Yes, yes, he mumbles, just coming.
He is there almost immediately, looking sheepish and a little
out of breath. He'd fallen asleep watching TV, he says with
nervous giggles. His haste in coming over may explain his
shorts and crumpled t-shirt, below-ankle socks and slippers –
and a display of hirsute milk-pale legs. He somehow looks
different from the Norris I'd encountered previously on my
walks. A young Asian of slight build and average height,
clean-faced and open. Short-cropped dark hair. I'd noticed his
habit of breaking into giggles no matter what the topic of
conversation – somewhat like the discordant windchime
hanging from my Jacaranda tree, a victim of capricious gusts.

~

I think I should keep the visit short - about forty minutes as
the breeze is getting to me. The sun had moved over to the
back of the house leaving us in shadow.

'So how you go, Norris?'

He sniffles and swipes the drip with the back of his hand.
I flinch.

'I moved back home because of coronavirus. Just tried
house sharing in Dandenong with a friend. Didn't work out.
But better at home.' Norris wriggles on his stool and laughs.
Asks me if I'm well, but in a childlike, timid manner.

I offer him a samosa and a glass of orange juice. He gives
the snack an uncertain *what's this* look. Takes a bite, nibbles,
and says 'Wow!'

'It's an Indian savoury,' I explain.

'But you're from South Africa, right? How come you eat Indian cookie?'

'That's because I have Indian blood. Grandparents shipped from India to South Africa with many others to work the fields of sugar cane for the British.'

'Yeah,' he said, 'like the Island people used to produce sugar in Queensland?'

'I guess so,' I said. Should read up on this, I think.

I learn that he was doing some kind of office work at a factory in Dandenong. Still reporting to work daily. Didn't know if he'd soon be told to work from home. Either way it was okay, he says. We speak about his parents having fewer and fewer offices to clean. And make do with some casual domestic cleaning. I spot their car parked at home more often now.

I pause abruptly in mid-sentence. Over Norris's shoulder, I notice two women walking briskly down Peter's driveway. My other neighbour. He's a ninety-four old post-war British migrant – so-called ten-pound Pom. His wife had, sadly, died a year ago in a nursing home. The women I recognise now are Peter's fifty-year-old daughter and his granddaughter. They stand at the foot of the stairs leading to the front door and call. When Peter, who seldom wears his hearing aid, fails to respond, the granddaughter runs up to the door, bangs on it once and scrambles back to her mother's side as if Peter would burst out like a grumpy old lion.

I try to disengage from the somewhat absurd drama and return to Norris, who by then is fiddling with his phone. He yawns, scratches his head and giggles some more. All the while we chat, I attempt to fathom why Norris wanted to *hang out* with me. Perhaps I should ask him straight out, I think.

'Hey, I haven't heard you partying with your friends lately. What's up?'

'Gave up going to church. Not interested.'

'Oh?'

'Yeah, all my church friends. Gave them up too.'

Now this was concerning. 'But why? So, who are your friends now?'

His face clouds over as if he is about to cry.

'Covid,' he blurted. 'Bad for health, for me, for mum and dad.'

That explains it, I conclude, and yet… At that moment, his parents return, park their red Toyota Corona in the street, get out and begin unpacking buckets, mops, and other cleaning paraphernalia from the boot. Norris jumps up and scurries off with a *thank you,* and a tentative bow.

Gosh, I hadn't noticed if Peter had heard all that commotion. Had he eventually emerged from his lost and lonely world to check who'd come knocking? Should call on him later, I resolve. Check how's he going.

The breeze in the Jacaranda tree was now asserting itself. I'm about to escape indoors when Norris comes rushing back. What now? I'm startled. Intrigued.

'Mum gave this for you,' he says brightly. 'From the garden.' He holds out a bunch of *bok choy,* freshly plucked, richly green.

I rest the stools and receive his mother's generosity.

'Thank you, and thank mum,' I say overcome with the unexpected.

Norris giggles, 'No worries.' I see his mother across the fence, smiling and waving.

'Hang out again, okay?' says Norris as he turns and walks away, his face bright with a look of satisfaction.

Dying Well

Ruby had been at her mother's bedside for several hours. An isolation ward at Monash Hospital in Melbourne. She felt distressed that others in the family couldn't visit because of Covid restrictions. None could relieve her. The strain on Ruby was telling. She sat frowning with hands clasped tightly between her knees, her eyes heavy with sleep.

'Someone has to be at her bedside, you know,' she muttered. 'Ma struggles to breathe. I feel helpless just watching her.'

At 94, Mrs Narain relished her physical stamina, her clarity of mind and joy of life. Even so her real wealth was her expansive family and friends.

On recent walks with Ruby, Mrs Narain tended to lag behind, which was most unlike her.

'What's happening, Ma?'

'Nothing's happening, Ruby. You go on, I'll keep up. Just feeling a little tired, you know. Maybe I haven't slept enough.' She had felt unusual bouts of tiredness recently but hadn't let on. Wear and tear of ageing had sneaked up on her.

When Mrs Narain began complaining of *short breath*, she was taken promptly to hospital emergency. It was absolutely the wrong time to be admitted with a respiratory condition.

Panic stations is how Ruby described it later. Hospital staff rushing around in protective gear, frantically securing all parts of the hospital for an anticipated influx of Covid-19 patients.

Ruby was given a gown and a face mask immediately. Mrs Narain was rushed through emergency and admitted to a ward without any patients. Total isolation. An unheard of experience for her.

'But why nobody visiting me, Ruby?' Mrs Narain fretted. She sorely missed her grandchildren, more especially Neelam, her only granddaughter. Neelam, now in her 20s, had basked in the nurturing love of her grandmother all her life. So, Ruby contrived a rare gift for her mother.

'Ma, let me help you to the window. There's a surprise out there.'

'What's that, eh?' Although weary and listless, Ma's face lit up. Even at her age, Mrs Narain loved fun and fooling around.

'I walked her a few shuffling steps to the window,' said Ruby 'pulling the oxygen tank along.'

'Look down there, Ma. Can you see the car park?' They were on the fourth level, and the carpark was a little way in the distance.

'Yah, I see lots of parked cars. But what surprise you saying? See no surprise,' she puzzled, straining her eyes. And then recognition.

'Ooooh yah,' she chuckled. Mrs Narain waves with delight seemingly unimpeded by the oxygen tubes in her nostrils.

Granddaughter Neelam had popped out from her car with a large colourful hand-made poster with just two bold images– a blood-red heart and beside it the letter U in red as well. Such demonstration of love in a time of Covid!

'Yah, there's my granddaughter,' she smiled sadly. 'I love you too, darling. I'll love you till I die.' She waved until exhausted.

The hospital was anxious to discharge Mrs Narain for fear she may contract Covid-19. It also meant an additional vacant bed.

The ward doctor addressed Ruby. 'We stabilised your mother. She's breathing a little better. It's best she's at home. Suggest you arrange for palliative care to visit. I'll give you a referral.' He was young and reassuring but clearly in need of bedrest himself.

'Thank you, doctor.' Ruby was greatly relieved.

'What's that he's saying?' Mrs Narain was hard of hearing but always keen to be fully informed about her health – a great believer in Devendra Vora's *Health in Your Hands*.

'Oh, going home, eh? How nice I'll be sleeping in my *own* bed in my *own* room.'

Sadly, once home, Mrs Narain's condition worsened. She became increasingly restless and suffered recurring bouts of breathlessness. Thankfully, for brief moments, she was coherent, able to recognise and speak with people. Although covid rules had to be observed, close family members could take turns in attending to her needs. Other well-wishers stood outside Mrs Narain's bedroom window, waved to her, threw kisses, and shouted encouragement.

'I can't make you better Mrs Narain,', said the palliative doctor in a kind voice, 'but I can make you comfortable.'

She nodded. If she understood the full import of that message, she was obviously stoic and accepting of her condition.

Ruby recalls her mother's final lucid moment.

'Say it louder Ma. I want to hear.' She recorded her mother's wise words on her phone.

'You know,' Mrs Narain whispered with effort, 'whenever the world becomes burdened with too many people, God finds ways of reducing the weight, like with sickness and floods. It says so in the Hindu scriptures.'

'You're talking about the Coronavirus, Ma?'

'Yah, that too. See how old people dying all over the world. I accept it's my time too.'

Mrs Narain had a virtual funeral. Her indomitable spirit probably rested now in some remote virtual world.

Death is for sure. But the question remains: Is *dying well* still a possibility in such unprecedented and uncertain times?

Covid Conversations

Conversation One

She: Amazing. I just heard Morrison say his lockdown saved 6000 lives or more so far. And they even prevented catastrophic numbers flooding the hospitals.

He: Is that so? Bloody amazing claim. And you believe that shit?

She: Sure, why not? It's to do with mathematical modelling, you know, by experts - even Daniel Andrews claims these are expert projections. You doubting it?

He: Yeah, like the scientific prediction that Labour would win the last elections hands down?

She: But that's different. I just can't talk to you these days. It's upsetting how negative you've become.

He: Sorry dear, I'm just asking? It's like Morrison went into the lockdown strategy saying: *Heads I win. Tails you lose.* Whatever the outcome, I'm the winner. In any case, that's how it sounds to me.

She: Just what ARE you on about?

He: All I'm saying is that even the best modelling is really guesswork in the end. It's to do with crunching numbers and saying this is what will happen. But the accuracy of the prediction is only as good as the data – and data is never enough or that reliable. It's just expert projection, you see. That's all. And what's more, straight-faced politicians like Morrison and Trump will say that there's glorious sunshine out there when, in reality, people are getting drenched in a winter storm.

She: Yeah, yeah, whatever. The thing is still, it hasn't turned out too badly, has it? At least, you've got to admit that.

Conversation Two

John: Isn't it simply great that not more people have died of Covid-19 in countries where governments acted quick and smart?

Peter: Oh? So, who are the thousands who *did* die?

John: Not sure. I think in Europe it was mostly the elderly living on their own or in aged care. And people already ill. They would have died in any case, that's the thing.

Peter: Yeah?

John: And oh, in New York lots of Blacks and Latinos, I'm told.

Peter: How come?

John: Can't really tell. Maybe they were the down-and-out poor, you know. People who didn't isolate and didn't care a damn, or just lived unhealthy lives on poor food.

Peter: That's interesting. And what about the health workers in the thick of things? I hear many have been infected or even died, like in Britain?

John: Right. They weren't mostly Whites though, were they? More likely migrants and people of colour who know no better. Like not having masks and things. Or not knowing how to use them.

Peter: Yeah, makes me wonder whose lives governments are mostly protecting.

Conversation Three

Brijh: You know, I sometimes feel like it's a blessing that Covid-19 has taken that many really old people, especially the ones in care homes.

Saku: But that's heartless. What a terrible thing to say. My mother's 82 and still enjoys life.

Brijh: But that's the point. Your mother lives with you, and things are always happening at home and in your large family. Isn't it? Her hearing is poor, but otherwise she's still doing things like pottering in the garden and fussing in the kitchen. You said that yourself. And the grandchildren light up her face.

Saku: Yeah, that's true. But what's your point?

Brijh: Well, have you ever been into one of the nursing homes for the elderly or visited an old person living alone in sub-standard apartments? No, I didn't think so. The thing is, you're so caught up with your own family, you simply never have the time or give it a thought.

Saku: But still, how can you wish them all dead? Surely each and every life is precious. God given.

Brijh: No, no. That's where people like you make a mistake. It's not *life* that's precious, but the *quality* of life.

The *quality of life*, Saku. It's what you see in your mother's eyes every day, and yet don't know it.

Saku: Oh well. I've not understood it in that way.

Brijh: Times have changed, you know. Few old people enjoy their twilight years like your mother. A clear mind and okay health. And gifted by close loving family.

Saku: Yea, my husband's mother lived far too long even though suffering pain and disability for years. Her eyes were failing, and her memory, mind you. No one in the family had the time to care for her – too busy with their own lives. So, they put her in a nursing home. A good one, according to my husband.

Brijh: Oh, but most of these places are privately run businesses out to make a killing. Old people rot in them, mostly die a slow death, losing their independence, identity, and dignity.

Saku: Come on Brijh, it may be bad for some sickly old folks, but you make out they're like being confined to hell or something. Abandoned by family. I've seen on TV old people in Care singing and dancing, and all smiles.

Brijh: Frankly, I don't wish to end up that way. God, not me. I hope not to lose my mind growing old. I need to know for myself when it's my time to go. Life in my hands that's my motto. To decide when and how I let go. Slow dying isn't for me.

Saku: You're just too much, Brijh. You may wish all you like, but in the end, God will decide how to dispose of you. Mark my word.

Conversation Four

Tony: The Premier is playing God. He acts like we are all his barnyard chooks needing protection from foxes.

Lily: That's a funny way to put it. For sure, beating the Coronavirus is more important than getting businesses moving again. I'm with the Premier all the way. To hell with the economy. It's the wealthy who's pushing for this, isn't it?

Tony: I wish it was that simple: People's health vs the economy.

Lily: No?

Tony: No. Definitely not. Look at it this way. Two sides of a coin with the community on the one side and economy on the other. The health of citizens, the nation, rests on many things coming together – thriving businesses, jobs for people which provides cash for survival (food, clothing, transport, shelter, recreation). It also buys you emotional wellbeing, purpose, social connection, family harmony. You see, *life* and *living* go together like a horse and carriage.

Lily: That's a mouthful, Tony. Sorry, but I don't quite get it, but keep going.

Tony: Well, the thing is, it's simply madness to want to save people from Covid-19 by imprisoning them in their homes and grinding the economy into the dirt. You know why?

Lily: Well, you tell me.

Tony: Even a ventilator pushed down your gullet may not prevent you dying – but at least it will be relatively quick and final. But financial stress and worry, want of sunlight and laughter, food insecurity, not knowing what's happening to your loved ones in nursing homes, not knowing if the virus will get you (even though you're faithfully following lockdown rules), that's dying of another kind. The slow but sure kind. When living becomes dying.

Lily: Jeez, now you've got me worried.

Tony: You *should* be worrying because if masses of people are driven to poverty and emotional distress, their immunity will suffer – and then we'll be easy prey to Mr Corona. Sitting ducks. The Premier better wise up before it's too late. Not to kill us with misplaced kindness. A bankrupt person in a bankrupt family in a bankrupt nation.

Conversation Five

Politician on TV: May I remind you we're all in it together.

Citizen: I'm sick of hearing that rubbish from the mouths of politicians. We're not all in it together, are we? Utter rubbish. Here, I can't pay my rent, don't know if I'll get another job, my bored kids bug me, and I'm prevented from visiting my old man in hospital. But the stupid politician's not in want of a good feed anytime, lives in his cushy mansion with his family AND, mind you, safe in his well-paid job. It's a lie they peddle. Makes me want to puke.

Politician on TV: Yes, yes. It isn't easy, I know. And it isn't going to get better any time soon. Accept it, right. Remember, we're all in it together.

Citizen: Piss off! (TV switched off)

Buddhist Encounters

Journey Of A Lifetime

Ten Thousand Miles Without a Cloud. That's the evocative title of a book by Sun Shuyun. The Buddhist notion of an enlightened mind in unbounded clarity is captured in this metaphor. The book covers the author's epic journey from China to India and back in the year 2000. In fact, Sun Shuyun traversed the inhospitable and ancient *Silk Route* across remote Central Asia. The Silk Road happens to be the fabled east-west highway from China to the Greco-Roman Empire used by traders, travellers, and armies for hundreds of years.

Sun Shuyun decided, quite deliberately, to retrace the 18 years journey of Xuanzang, a Chinese Buddhist monk in the seventh century. This remarkable young monk had set his mind on finding and bringing back to China the true essence of the *dharma* from India. It was mere chance that, while studying at Oxford University, Shuyun learnt that Xuanzang had been a real human being who had lived during the Tang dynasty – not just a fictitious character of the popular Chinese children's story *The Monkey King*.

Buddhism was what her late grandmother had clung to with hope and fervour all through her personal losses during the dark days of Mao's Cultural Revolution. At the time, Sun

Shuyun says she was taught that Buddhism 'was something bad' and, consequently, '95% of the monasteries in China were destroyed'. She herself as a teenager, harassed and ridiculed her grandmother no end. As an adult, however, a mixture of guilt and curiosity drove her to find out more about Buddhism and Xuanzang. She adopted this as her personal mission and set about the arduous journey with unwavering fervour.

~

Sun Shuyun's account is truly inspiring, illuminating and absorbing. Her writing is rich, elegant, and scholarly. The story is told simultaneously on four levels: historical, cultural, spiritual, and personal. The experiences, reflections and discoveries of Sun Shuyun unfold in the book, page after page, now intersecting with and now diverging from that of Xuanzang. Buddhism was understood and practised in many varied ways across the ancient silk route – from a form that was pristine, rational, and liberating to practices that were invested with gods, demons, rituals, and superstition. The Buddha was a mere mortal to some and an all-powerful god to others. For Sun Shuyun, the very impermanence of life is reflected in the relentless rise, decline and wanton destruction of nations, peoples, cities, and civilisations (Buddhism included) all along the Silk Road, over the centuries. In fact, Sun Shuyun tells us that she was about to enter Afghanistan at the very time that the priceless Buddhas of Bamiyan, 175 feet in height, were blown up by the Taliban in a dramatic and appalling manner. One of the great ironies, according to Sun Shuyun, is that Buddhism disappeared in India, the birthplace of Buddha, for centuries virtually without a trace – 'a darkness shrouded Buddhist India'. There was even a belief that Buddha was simply a figure from Indian mythology – that is, until Alexander Cunningham, a British Army engineer, unearthed incontrovertible archaeological evidence of Buddhism in about 1850 in places like Sarnath, Bodh Gaya and Kushinagar. He was apparently inspired by numerous clues in Xuanzang's famous journal written some thirteen hundred years earlier. The journal, *A Record of the Western Regions* is credited for the rediscovery (as recently as about 150 years ago) of Buddhism as it flourished in India and Central Asia in the centuries following the death of the Buddha.

A further irony noted by Sun Shuyun is that Buddha became enlightened, taught his first sermon, and died in Bihar, a state in India still notorious for its endemic poverty, repression, injustice, and lawlessness. In fact, we are told that Bihar is a corruption of the Buddhist term *vihara* – meaning sanctuary or monastery.

As a woman travelling on her own, Sun Shuyun faced many risks and challenges on her journey lasting a year. However, her hurdles were nowhere near the trials and tribulations endured by Xuanzang as he traversed rivers in flood, desolate snow-covered mountains, relentless deserts and extremes of weather. Many a time he was waylaid by ferocious robbers on the Silk Road. Both Sun Shuyun and Xuanzang indicate genuine interest in the peoples they encountered all along their journey. It must have certainly required much boldness and courage for them to engage strangers in unfamiliar foreign places. Hence, their fascinating descriptions of peoples and their customs, prejudices and struggles in distant worlds, possibly far removed from any exotic places we may have visited. Theirs are stories told and reflected upon with enormous candour, sympathy, and wisdom.

~

Sun Shuyun writes about fascinating Buddhist antiquity in the form of statues, reliefs, manuscripts, and murals, some still in excavated caves, stupas, and temples. But most of these she found in museums in places like Peshawar, New Delhi, and Benares. Of course, the British Museum has one of the biggest collections of Buddhist artefacts, since the British were one of the greatest plunderers of antiquity! Interestingly, Sun Shuyun writes about the earliest origins of Buddhist statues in Gandhara (now somewhere across Pakistan and Afghanistan) with obvious ancient Greek influence since the people who created them were descendants of the armies of Alexander the Great. For instance, the very early sculptured heads of the Buddha were depicted with curly hair tied in a knot on top, whereas the Buddha, being an Indian, would have had straight black hair.

~

On a personal note, Sun Shuyun reflects on her own childhood as a girl and an 'unwanted daughter' in a China where 'ignorance was considered a virtue in women'. In her book, she recollects snippets of her growing up in a small town in China during Mao's Cultural Revolution. She writes about the hardships, fear, repression, and betrayals endured by her family and community, her own destructive excesses as a Red Guard and, above all, how her grandmother (who loved her dearly) was ridiculed and shunned for clinging to her faith in Guanyin, the Bodhisattva of compassion. Her journey, then, at one level is a bold statement on behalf of women the world over, oppressed and abused over generations. At another level, Sun Shuyun bears witness to the infinite capacity of humans to inflict pain and destruction, to suffer, endure and to triumph. In the process, she attempts to make amends for her total own lack of compassion and generosity during the Cultural Revolution – especially towards her family. She wonders if she had finally understood the essence of the *dharma* and if, at heart, she was now a 'Buddhist'.

~

Xuanzang ended his journey in 645 AD in China where he had started. So does Sun Shuyun, more than 1300 years later. The very first thing she does on her return is to pay homage at her grandmother's grave. 'I placed on her grave bananas, oranges and grapes that I had brought her, the simple things she never tasted in life'.

Recollections

(Buddhist retreat, Anglesea: November 2005)

Listen! What do you hear
In the stillness of the night?
I hear but the sound
Of silence and emptiness!
And what do you see?
Ah! The tall shadow of Sayadaw,
Cast by candlelight.
I see darkly visible hulks
Of sitting Yogis
And gliding ghost-like,
Walking meditators
Shrouded in
Awesome stillness.

Yet listen again:
What is it you hear?
Ah! From the depth of silence
Come mutterings
Of many minds,
Beginners' minds,
Silently enduring pain,

Stepping out on the arduous path
To Mount Kailash.
The frozen wind howls and mocks,
Three days no end,
Relentless
Night and day
Across a Tibetan plateau.
Searing
Through fissures in my mind

Assailing the senses
As I sit and walk, walk and sit,
Through weary hours from sunrise to dusk.
Will a peaceful mind ever arise!

Ah! The Emptiness of Suffering.

On the fourth and final day of the retreat, as we sat for dawn meditation, a deep mist arose shrouding the world around. The trees were miraculously still, the ground wet with dew, and the crisp air peppered with myriad invisible birdcalls. My heart soared as my previous afflictions evaporated, and peace arose in me as my meditation practice came good – at least for the moment.

Then came the news that the two-week-old grandchild of one of the practitioners had taken seriously ill, and she departed in haste, sobbing. Our distress was palpable as we chanted *metta*.

But soon the mist cleared, and the morning sky turned a blissful blue. The warmth of the sun was tempered by a gentle breeze. And Aussie flies returned, troublesome and all too familiar.

Presently we packed and departed on our various ways. The four-day retreat was effectively over, insubstantial as the mist. The Coastal Forest Lodge was relegated once more to its pristine state – a cluster of silent buildings on a vacant landscape.

A Never-Ending Story

Swish! Swish! Sweeesh! I'm momentarily distracted by the distinct sound of someone sweeping the path outside the meditation hall, at the Buddhist Centre in Malvern. It strikes me that sweeping pathways can often be a never-ending story. It certainly is at the Centre.

At times the paths are heavily strewn with leaves and seed pods from the many eucalyptus trees nearby, as well as with pink flowers of the oleander bushes. This is more evident after a spell of wind or heavy rain.

Some Sunday mornings, I get to the centre much before the formal sitting to secure a parking spot. I have time then to pick up the broom myself. I quite enjoy sweeping with a firm fan-shaped reed broom traditionally used in South-East Asian countries like Thailand. Only the most stubborn leaves can withstand the thrust and push of this remarkable broom. When the work is done, I usually survey the paved paths, now spotless. I feel pleased with my diligence and effort. But even as I return the broom to its accustomed place, and proceed to the meditation hall, the eucalyptus and oleander continue to do the thing that comes naturally to them – blissfully shedding yellowing leaves and spent flowers.

On one occasion, as I was so blissfully absorbed in sweeping (the broom, the path and me almost melding), a meditator walking past called out: *Hey, you know a disciple of the Buddha apparently gained enlightenment while sweeping his monastery.* Of course, I smiled and thanked him for his noble encouragement. But I had my doubts. Fat hope of it ever happening a second time!

I recall the daily ritual at Wat Pah Nanachat in northern Thailand, the forest monastery established especially for aspiring western monks, by the internationally renowned Venerable Ajahn Chah. I had visited this forest retreat over a few days in 2000. I awoke each morning at first light to the familiar sound of many brooms sweeping. And there were enough leaf-strewn dirt paths beneath the sun-speckled forest canopy for a whole team of monks and novices to practise mindful sweeping to their hearts' delight. I, too, was momentarily swept up by this very eminently simple and practical means of mindfulness practice.

Meditation practitioners will perhaps agree that purifying the mind of unwholesome thoughts is a never-ending process. A lifelong endeavour. Fortunately for us, there always will be paths ready and waiting to be swept.

Acknowledgments

This collection of stories took several months to write, compile, and edit. Many people generously helped bring it to a publishable standard

My special appreciation to Professor Chris Goddard for writing the Foreword which skilfully contextualises the book in the landscape of reflections, drawing readers' interests to read the stories. I also gratefully acknowledge his time in carefully scrutinising the manuscript and ferreting out the most elusive errors.

Kieran Carroll, a longstanding friend, and renowned playwright has been a constant source of support and encouragement to me. His generosity of time in perusing early drafts and his insightful feedback is greatly appreciated. So too his back-cover endorsement.

I must acknowledge the unwavering assistance of Robert New for cover design and formatting. And Tale Publishing for publishing the book.

Once again, an enormous hug to my wife (Neerosh) for her enduring interest in my writing, for patiently reading and editing my first drafts and for promoting my books.

My appreciation to friends and members of my writers' group who have contributed in many different ways to this publication.

Books come alive only when they are read. Readers, you are my greatest asset.

About the Author

Bala Mudaly is an Indian South African, born in Durban in 1938. Chronic job insecurity and political harassment compelled him to migrate to Australia in 1988 with his wife.

He retired as a clinical psychologist from Monash Health in Melbourne in Dec 2018 at the age of 80.

His debut collection of poems and short stories set in Australia, *Colours of Hope and Despair*, was launched in 2018 and still available on Kindle. He has also had a short story, *Self-Inflected Pain of the Writer's Kind*, published in the Victorian Writer, a quarterly writers' magazine. The author has contributed short pieces to a fortnightly online publication of the University of KwaZulu Natal in Durban, the Creative Network Magazine. As an amateur writer, he has workshopped almost all his creative writings in a Writers Group sponsored by the City of Monash public library service. His memoir, *Colour-Coated Identity*, was his most ambitious creative non-fiction project published in 2021.

Currently, the author is working on a novel with the tentative title: *Nothing's For Sure*. Its theme is the challenges of friendships and family relationships in post-apartheid South Africa beyond the constraints of race and colour.

Contact Bala at: bala.mudaly@gmail.com

www.ingramcontent.com/pod-product-compliance
Lightning Source LLC
Chambersburg PA
CBHW061925130726
47909CB00012B/1089